HEARTSTRINGS

TONI BLAKE

For my parents,
who always supported my creativity and encouraged me to chase
my dreams.

CHAPTER ONE

*J*osie Bell put one worn cowboy boot in front of the other as she walked up a flat, dusty South Carolina lane toward her childhood home. In her right hand, she carried a beat-up guitar case. In her left, an equally beat-up duffle bag.

She tossed a glance over her shoulder at the old pickup truck that had carried her all the way from Nashville, but hadn't quite made it the last hundred yards. Not the classic Chevy's fault—she'd neglected to notice the gas needle on E. Practical concerns had never been her strong suit.

The dirt lane gave way to a white picket fence she remembered well, and a cozy, shaded lawn on the other side. Towering oaks draped with Spanish moss bent large branches over the house like protective arms. "One day one of those branches is going to break off in a storm and come crashing through the roof," her sister, Daphne, had recently said to her on the phone. Daphne had never loved the house the way Josie had. The house was the one good thing about coming back here. It was like a safety net, a place to catch her after a fall.

1

She stepped up to the white gate, raising her gaze to the signpost beside it. The two-story clapboard home had been built in a time when people gave houses names. Her great grandparents had called this one Rosebud. It wasn't so grand a structure as most houses that sported such names—but it was well kept, warm, and loved. Cottage green shutters and doors, accompanied with bits of salmon pink trim, served as the perfect accents on the white weatherboard background.

Her whole life, people had called the home by its given name. It was never "Josie's house" or "Daphne's" or "the Bell place." Friends would say, "There's a bonfire tonight at Rosebud," or "Pick you up at Rosebud at six." It had been a gathering place, bustling with life.

And maybe it was crazy, but the house looked a little sad to her right now. Possibly because no one lived in it anymore. Or maybe because of the ugly *For Sale* sign in the front yard. She'd never been happier that the house resided at the end of a private lane where the lack of traffic made the sign, to her way of thinking, mostly useless.

First things first—she lowered her guitar and bag to the ground, unlatched the gate, and walked to the metal realty sign. Pulling it up from the yard, she carried it to the side of the house and leaned it against the foundation, out of sight, making it *completely* useless. *There, that's better.*

Then, wiping off her hands, she reached into the back pocket of her blue jeans, pulled out her cell phone, and dialed the number on the sign.

"Sandy Listerman," said a voice on the other end after only one ring.

"Sandy, it's Daphne Rawley," she lied. Most people couldn't tell her and her sister apart on the phone—which had been awkward and even occasionally embarrassing as teenagers, but seemed pretty handy right now.

"Daphne—what can I do for you?"

"We've decided to take the house off the market."

"Oh—I—uh...I thought..."

I thought you'd moved your parents to a condo in Myrtle Beach near you and your husband because they're too old for the upkeep and don't need such a big place anymore. Josie heard all that in Sandy's awkward stammer—since surely she'd been filled in on this information. "I know, I know," Josie said, taking on Daphne's usual matter-of-fact tone. "But my younger sister's come home unexpectedly and will be living there indefinitely."

She could feel Sandy's confusion. Sandy probably didn't know there *was* a sister. "I, um...you realize you have a month left on your current contract, Daphne."

"Yes, of course—but it's necessary. I'm sorry, and thanks. We'll call you the next time we need a realtor. Take care now." And then she disconnected.

Before she'd left home for Nashville seven years ago, she couldn't have done something so bold and without a second thought. But Music City had chewed her up and spit her back out, leaving her a different person, in some ways for the better and in some for the worse. It wasn't easy to chase a dream, but she'd chased hers. It was even harder to *give up* on a dream, but she'd finally done that, too.

She didn't have a plan. She didn't know what she was going to do with her life now, how she would manage to keep Rosebud, or how she'd face her past and the things—and people—she'd left behind. But she had no other choice. With no place else to go, Josie Bell had come home to Sassafras, South Carolina, out of money, out of luck—and out of gas.

∼

TANNER ROSE STOOD next to his brother Jace, on the beach in

3

khakis and an untucked white shirt—standard best man wear for a casual beach wedding these days. "Jace, you may kiss your perty bride," said Pete Haggard, better known in Sassafras as Salty Pete, and the proprietor of the open-air seafood shack a stone's throw away across the sand. Pete was no one's idea of a clergyman, but he'd gotten ordained online just for this occasion. Tanner's mother had balked—until Jace reminded her how little family his bride, Shelby, had, and that her waitressing job at Salty Pete's had created an unlikely relationship between her and the usually crusty old man.

Tanner applauded, along with the rest of the small crowd, as Jace took Shelby's face between his hands for the kiss. And it was a hell of a kiss.

He was happy for his brother. And happy for their eldest brother, Rick, who'd recently announced his own engagement to his girlfriend of several years, Mia. Not a quick mover by nature—too controlling for that—Rick had only popped the question after Jace had met and proposed to Shelby in a matter of mere weeks. Mia had grown tired of waiting, Tanner suspected. And was a saint for putting up with his good-hearted—but again, controlling—big bro, as far as he was concerned.

Most people were a little surprised that Jace, a reformed ladies' man, was the first of the Rose brothers to walk down the aisle, but as he and Shelby were pronounced husband and wife, the bigger surprise to Tanner was that he himself would be the *last*. At thirty-two, he was the youngest of the three, so maybe it made sense—except that he'd originally thought he'd found the girl he would marry before he'd turned eighteen. They'd spent seven years together, in no hurry, being sensible and saving a little money, getting established, making their parents happy by not rushing. And that kind of longevity had definitely made it seem like he'd be the one to say *I do* long before his brothers. Funny how things changed.

"Hey there, cutie!" He turned to see the woman he'd been dating for a while, Ashlynn, approach as the wedding ended and the happy couple started greeting their guests. Her long, blond hair whipped in the sea breeze.

"Hey." He tried to smile. But it irked him that she called him cutie. Especially in a crowd. He wasn't even sure why.

"You did great!"

His entire job had been to hand Jace the ring. "Thanks." Ashlynn tended to be overly enthusiastic about things.

She pulled out her cell phone, stretched out her arm, and said, "Let's take a wedding selfie."

He leaned in and obliged, even as her hair blew in both their faces. He wasn't really much of a selfie guy, but he knew girls liked that sort of thing.

"I always thought this was a drab little beach," she said of the crescent-shaped swath of sand behind Salty Pete's, "but it's prettier for a wedding than I thought. Would *you* ever want to get married on a beach?"

Tanner blinked. He'd always known Ashlynn wanted their relationship to progress more than he did—but she didn't usually ask questions this pointed. "Um, never thought about it."

Just then, his phone notified him of a text—saved by the buzz. He quickly extracted it from his pocket to find a message from Ronnie Tucker, a friendly business competitor. Tanner and Ronnie both ran small construction companies, and sent work each other's way when one of them had more than they could handle.

Hey bud, want a job? Lady needs an estimate on some home remodeling and sounded in a rush. I can't get to her until next month.

Tanner texted back. *Depending on the size of the job, I can do it.* He had crews busy with other projects—it was March, and spring in South Carolina brought new construction—but his workload wasn't at full capacity.

Ronnie sent a quick reply. *She wanted me to stop by today at four. I know it's a Saturday, but if it's good for you, I'll tell her I'm sending somebody. 11946 Cedar Highway.*

Got it—I'll be there. Thanks for the rec, buddy.

He didn't want to skip out on his brother's wedding reception, but given that the whole affair was small, it would probably be wrapping up by then. And he should probably feel guilty about skipping out on Ashlynn, too, but if today had put weddings on her mind a little too much, maybe it was best they didn't spend the whole afternoon together.

AFTER CHANGING into a pair of blue jeans and workboots later that day, Tanner drove toward the address he'd keyed into his cell phone's map app. Addresses along rural stretches were sometimes hard for the GPS to pinpoint, and as he neared this one, it occurred to him that...the area felt familiar. A little too close for comfort to a place from his past. And he didn't like dredging up old memories.

But like it or not, those memories came even closer when the GPS told him to turn right, leaving Cedar Highway— onto an old flat gravel lane he'd once known very well. And it hit him that the lane had never had a name—it was more of a mile-long shared driveway that led to five or six houses, all set far apart. "Damn lane should have a name," he muttered under his breath. If the damn lane had a name, he'd have recognized it, known where he was going. And he'd have asked more questions.

As each of the houses along the path turned out *not* to be 11946, he considered turning his pickup around, calling

Ronnie, and telling him he couldn't make it after all. Because even just dealing with her parents or her sister would be awkward. And *they* clearly knew that, too, since they'd called Ronnie and not him.

And then there it was, the last house, sitting at the end of the unnamed lane, the late afternoon sun shining on it like a spotlight, a spotlight on his past, a spotlight on the one time in his life he'd ever allowed his heart to be broken, something he never intended to let happen again.

Yep, this was a bad idea. He was going to turn the truck around and leave.

Only as he cruised slowly forward, his eyes stuck on *another* truck—a 1958 Chevy pickup, faded cornflower blue, that he and his dad had restored as a twenty-first birthday present over ten years ago. He'd never thought he'd see that truck again—and was so dumbstruck by the sight that he let his own roll slowly past it, until easing to a stop before a sagging white picket fence and the sign rising above the gate that said *Rosebud*.

That truck could only mean one thing. Josie was home.

The notion clamped like a vise around his heart, making it hard to breathe.

Which was ridiculous. *You shouldn't feel that way. You shouldn't feel any damn way about her at all. You've been apart as long as you were together. You picked up the pieces and moved on.*

Of course, the tightness in his chest right now refuted that claim.

But he'd just never expected this. The truck. The house. Or...her.

And then there she was, emerging from the shade like a ghost of Sassafras past, exiting the gate to greet him. And damn, she looked beautiful as ever. And double damn, it was too late to leave—that window of opportunity had closed. Even as his heart beat like a drum against his ribcage, there was nothing to do but face the music—the music that was Josie.

He got out, slammed the door on his late model Ford, and strode toward the petite brunette who'd climbed into that old truck and driven right out of his life without a word seven years ago.

CHAPTER TWO

*a*s Josie took bold steps toward the contractor, he began to seem familiar. And then he became... Tanner. Right before her eyes. How could this be?

Her stomach lurched and she feared she'd be sick. What the hell was he doing here? And why didn't he even look surprised? Or affected? And how affected did *she* look? She tried her damnedest to steel herself, appear as cool and unruffled as he did. "Tanner?" It didn't work, she knew, could feel it. She sounded positively aghast.

"Yep," he replied. Stone-cold casual. But maybe not *wholly* unaffected. Possibly a low-level anger floated underneath that. She couldn't blame him. She couldn't blame him at all.

But she had no idea what to say. "I...I...what are you doing here?"

"Ronnie Tucker was too busy, so he referred *me*."

She swallowed. "He didn't mention that."

Her ex-fiancé gave a brusque nod. "Not always the best with details, Ronnie." Then he pointed over his shoulder to his 4x4 pickup. "Maybe best I leave and let you call somebody else."

And then he started to go—just like that. Seven years apart and...well, again, though, she couldn't blame him for just walking away. That was what *she'd* done, after all.

Yet she heard herself say, "Wait."

He'd already turned to go, but stopped. Looked back.

His eyes were as blue as ever. But other things had changed: His shoulders had broadened—he'd filled out, grown up, grown older; he was a man now. His once-light hair looked darker. His face sported stubble.

And despite any differences in either of them, their entire history stood between them, still connecting them. She couldn't let him leave without at least asking, "How are you?" The words came out softer than planned, little more than a whisper in the stillness of a rural coastal spring afternoon.

"I'm...fine, Josie." He said it with a certain sureness—clearly he wanted her to know that he really *was* fine. Fine without her.

"I'm glad." And she truly was. She'd never wanted to hurt him. Leaving had nearly killed her—but she'd had to do it.

"I could ask you the same thing you asked me," he said. "What are you doing here?"

She drew in her breath, blew it back out. Big question.

But maybe she owed him the simplest answer—not the one she would give other people, the one about missing home, missing family, deciding Nashville wasn't for her. For Tanner, the unvarnished truth. "I gave up," she said.

His jaw dropped. Just slightly. She'd thrown him with that brutal honesty. Thrown him enough that he said nothing.

So she went on. "Ran out of money, ran out of options, ran out of...believing that I could make it." Then she let out a self-deprecating laugh. "Only took me seven years to figure out what everybody else already knew."

He still said nothing. And she was almost sorry she'd dipped that low—reminding him that she'd been the one and only person who'd ever thought she had what it took to become a country music star. But it was the truth. If she'd listened back then, she'd be a whole lot better off now. She'd be Tanner's wife. She'd have a beautiful life.

And on a lark, she decided to put the rest out there—say what she'd been wanting to say for years now. "Tanner, this is long overdue, and maybe it won't count for much—but I'm sorry. So sorry. I never should have left. Especially the way I did."

His eyes dropped to the ground. His lips pressed flat together. Still stone-cold, no emotion whatsoever. That wasn't the Tanner she remembered. Had her departure changed him that much? Or was that giving herself too much credit? Maybe this was just part of that growing up and getting older thing she'd noticed—maybe he'd changed because sometimes people just do.

"It's in the past," he said. "Let's not dredge it up."

She wasn't sure if that equated to accepting her apology or just ignoring it, but either way, she had no choice but to quietly say, "All right."

Then his gaze flitted toward the house. He looked uncertain. "What is it you're wanting done here anyway?"

"I was thinking of adding some bathrooms," she told him.

He blinked. "Why?"

She looked to the old home too. "Well, Mom and Dad have moved into a condo on Myrtle Beach, and they've been trying to sell the place for a year without even a nibble—so I thought rather than just letting it fall completely apart that maybe I'd turn it into an inn. The Rosebud Inn." Letting her gaze flit from the house back to him, she cast a hopeful smile. "Isn't that a nice idea?"

He tossed her a frank look. "It's the worst idea I've ever heard."

Flinching, she drew back and did some blinking of her own. "What do you mean?"

He sighed, shifted his weight from one workboot to the other. "Josie, Sassafras can't support an inn. It's a tiny town with virtually no tourism. If we needed an inn, there'd be one already."

Crap, he made a deflatingly good point. Not that she'd be deterred that easily. "But maybe it's like in *Field of Dreams*—if I build it, they will come."

Another deprecating sigh from her handsome ex. "And you'd make a terrible innkeeper."

At this, her eyes went wide. "Well, that's a mean thing to say."

He shrugged. "It's an *honest* thing to say. Last I checked, you like to follow your whims, come and go as you please. An innkeeper is pretty much tied to an inn. Do you want to spend your life being a glorified maid—washing people's sheets and towels, cleaning their bathrooms, making sure you're here at all hours of the day and night to take care of whatever they need?"

Wow. Okay. The truth was, she'd only come up with the inn idea today after taking Rosebud off the market. But Tanner made such an existence sound pretty miserable. And like one more thing she would fail at. She spoke quietly, defeated. "I was only trying to think of a way to keep the house, make it useful, fill it with new life. And...a way to make some money. Since I don't have any."

He narrowed his gaze on her. "How were you planning to pay for the remodeling?"

Oh boy. Now it was she who sighed, her glance dropping to her boots. "I'm...not sure." She felt like an idiot. "All I've ever wanted to do was sing, so this is...a whole new way of approaching life for me. I was trying to think outside the box. But I guess inside the box is a safer place for my brain."

When she least expected it, Tanner used one bent finger to lift her chin.

Her eyes met his.

And an old familiar desire gathered in her solar plexus. Just from that—that tiny touch. And the meeting of their eyes.

"There's nothing wrong with your brain, Jos," he said, his voice gentler now but still as deep. "It just doesn't work exactly like everybody else's."

She swallowed back old emotions. Tanner had always understood her. Understood her and supported her and taken up for her. He got that she lived in the moment and had trouble planning. That her passions drove her far more than practicality. In high school, he'd understood—even when their teachers didn't—that she simply hadn't been able to focus on completing a boring assignment because she'd been busy writing a song. And now he understood that her passion for saving the house had gotten way ahead of the practical concerns behind the wish.

"Thank you," she softly replied. It hadn't served her particularly well in life, but she'd never figured out how to think and operate the way other people did. Which was surely at least part of the reason she was back here in Sassafras with barely two guitar picks to rub together, and an empty gas tank on top of it. "You're the only one who ever really got me."

He darted his glance away—it was as if he'd touched a hot stove. And it told her with certainty: He *did* still have emotions about her—strong ones. He just didn't want to let himself feel them.

And rather than acknowledge what she'd just said, instead he looked out over Rosebud's vast yard and told her—his voice a little more distant, same as his eyes, "Would make more sense if you did something that has to do with your music."

The suggestion caught her off-guard—given that her music was the one and only thing that had ultimately driven them apart.

She'd known she'd never be able to live a happy, content, satisfied life if she didn't try to make it in Nashville, and he'd been unwilling to uproot his life and go with her. So she'd gone without him. Without even a goodbye.

Because that would have been too painful.

So she'd just run, literally snuck off under the cover of darkness one spring night, driving the truck he'd given her on her twenty-first birthday all the way to Tennessee before allowing herself to stop and look back.

The suggestion threw her for other reasons, too. She just told him she'd given up. For all *he* knew, she was fed up with music now. Of course, she wasn't—it remained the biggest part of her soul—but how did he know that? Or maybe… that was one more way in which he still understood her. Some connections couldn't be severed—even by time and distance.

Yet she reminded him, "I've already tried that."

"In Nashville," he said. "Not here."

She wasn't sure what he was proposing. "If Sassafras can't even support an inn, it probably isn't going to make me the next Miranda Lambert."

But now Tanner was looking around some more—and even letting himself into the yard through the front gate. So she followed. Followed him as he crossed the wide lawn down to the sloped area that led to a flat, wide clearing where they and their friends had built bonfires as teenagers. And in fact, every step they took reminded her of her past, *their* past, a relationship much of which had taken place here on the expansive grounds of Rosebud—the upkeep once a hobby for her father until age had snuck up on him and turned it into more of a job than a joy.

She wondered if Tanner was walking down memory lane along with her—but concluded his mind had stayed on business when he stopped in the middle of the clearing and said, "This might sound crazy, but what if you put a stage here? Like right here, where I'm standing."

She blinked her confusion. It *did* sound a little crazy. "Why? So I can sing for an audience of shrubs and trees?"

"I'm thinking of benches on the hills leading down. In a semi-circle. Make it an amphitheater."

She remained just as bewildered—benches or not. "Who will sit on them? Rabbits and squirrels?"

"Listen," he said, finally turning to face her, "Sassafras may not need an inn, but it could use a music venue. Singers and bands approach Rick all the time wanting to play in the bar." His older brother owned the Rose Tavern in town. "But it's really too small for that. And Wally Devlin's bluegrass band and some other acts play at festivals in the summer, and he's told me they feel like they could draw in a regular crowd if they had someplace to do it. Denver Ellis, too—he does nineties country covers but has to drive an hour or two to find a bar that hires live music acts, and competition for the work is stiff. Too many musicians—not enough places with live music, especially country."

She bit her lip, thinking it through. "So you're suggesting…"

"An outdoor music venue. For you and anybody else you want to book. Every weekend if it takes off. You charge ten or twenty bucks a head and take part of the cut. Maybe make some money off concessions, too." Then he pointed up the hill, toward the lane. "There's plenty of room to park out there, and I could add a gate direct to the stage, separate from the one that leads up the front walk—put in some steps coming down." Next he pointed to an old gatehouse mostly used for storage her whole life. "That's your office and ticket window right there."

It was clear to Josie that Tanner's creative builder mind had taken off on this the same way her own mind sometimes did when a new song started buzzing around inside her head. But..."You think I could make enough off of this to, you know, live. Comfortably?"

He shrugged. "Maybe it's a long shot—I don't know. But like *you* said—build it and they'll come. Worst case scenario —it's a place to play music and hold events at least from time to time, and it wouldn't take much to get it up and running if we kept the construction simple."

At this, however, another sigh snuck out. "But how am I going to pay for *that*—simple or not?"

Tanner looked over at her—another electric meeting of eyes that made her heart flutter, along with other sensitive body parts. "Tell you what—pay me as you can. A cut of the profits until it's covered. No profits—I don't get paid. If it turns out to be a dumb idea, it's my fault and I'll take the hit." He winked. "How's that work for ya?"

He'd actually winked. She wasn't sure how he'd gone from the stern, no-nonsense, non-smiling Tanner who'd driven up to her gate a few minutes ago to this happier, kinder, sweeter Tanner—much closer to the Tanner she'd fallen in love with—but she liked this one far more.

And she had no idea if his plan made any sense or not—in terms of actually providing an income. But she loved it just the same. She loved the notion of still singing and playing her guitar, and maybe even having people come to listen. And she loved the vision in her mind of Rosebud bustling with people and excitement and music. She'd left Nashville feeling, woefully, that that part of her life was behind her, that it had to be—but maybe it could exist here, at home, just in a new way.

"It sounds...amazing," she confessed. "Only...one thing?"

He'd resumed looking around the space again, clearly making mental construction plans. Now he returned his glance to her. "What's that?"

"Why are you doing this? Why are you suddenly being so nice to me? After...well, everything."

He almost hid the flinch, but not quite. She'd just brought him back to reality—to *their* reality—which maybe he'd somehow forgotten there for a minute. He dropped his gaze, then raised it back, but this time toward the house. "You're right that this place is too special to let it fall apart. Maybe I like the idea of having a hand in saving it. That's all."

Still, her question had clearly injected a fresh bit of tension into the air. No matter how you sliced it, she'd still heartlessly left him seven years ago without a word since. "If...if you go home and think about this and change your mind, Tanner...well, I wouldn't blame you."

He regarded her from beneath shaded lids. Yeah, it had been easy to ignore their past for a few minutes, but it still hung there, lingering, unresolved. "I won't," he said. "I keep my commitments."

Ouch. But she deserved that. She deserved far worse, in fact.

"I'm gonna head home and start drawing up some plans for a stage, and I'll be back in a couple days to show you some options and take some measurements."

She nodded. "Okay—sounds good." *And sounds positively surreal, all things considered.* An hour ago, she was expecting a random contractor to be giving her estimates for bathrooms, and now her ex, the love of her life, was building an amphitheater in her yard.

Of course, while he was drawing up plans, she'd have to

do some work of her own—namely getting the family to sign off on what would surely sound like a hare-brained scheme. And to do that...

"Tanner, before you go...um, any chance you have a gas can on you? Like with some gas in it?" She winced as she asked.

They'd started ascending the hill together, and now he glanced toward the old blue pickup. "That's why the truck is so far down the lane?"

She gave a quiet, sheepish nod.

And he replied with a small head shake that said *typical Josie*. "No gas can," he answered on a sigh, "but I've got a small hose in the bed. I can siphon some out of my tank into yours."

My hero. She almost said it, but bit her tongue. It was true, though. Even after all this time and all her mistakes. The last thing she'd expected upon coming home was for Tanner Rose to come to her rescue—but there was no one on this earth who she'd rather be saved by.

CHAPTER THREE

*D*riving away from Josie and Rosebud felt like waking up from a dream. Or a nightmare—he wasn't sure which and all the lines had blurred at the moment. The last time he'd been this shellshocked was... well, when she left. The day he'd gone to her house and found out from her mother that she'd discarded her engagement ring on her bedside table with a note saying she was heading west in the old pickup, looking for fame and fortune in Nashville.

It had been the one bone of contention between them always. He'd encouraged her singing—she was talented and had a beautiful voice—but when she'd wanted him to chuck all his plans and dreams in order to follow hers, he couldn't do it.

"You can build things anywhere," she'd pleaded. "But I need to be in Nashville if I'm serious about making something of myself."

"I already have a company *here*," he'd replied. "And face it, Jos, no matter how talented you are, what are the chances?

For every success story out of Nashville, there are probably a thousand broken hearts."

Her response had been to write a song called "A Thousand Broken Hearts and One of 'em's Mine." The lyrics had told the story of someone who ensured their failure by not even trying, by letting life pass them by rather than chasing their dream.

And *his* response had been to feel hurt and insulted. Hearing that she considered life here in Sassafras, as his wife, the equivalent of letting life pass her by had stung.

They'd both been twenty-four at the time—and they'd both been single-minded and determined and sure they knew what they wanted and what was best. But he felt a hell of a lot older and wiser *now*.

Less than a year after that conversation, she'd be gone, changing everything about what he'd thought the rest of his life would be. While most guys wanted to play the field and take their time working toward marriage, he'd been more than happy to have found the love of his life early, content to settle down young, start a family, continue building his business. In the end, all that was left of those plans was the business. And he valued what he'd grown there, having come from a family of entrepreneurs and starting the company at the age of twenty-one. But some days he wondered if he'd made the wrong decision.

After driving aimlessly for a little while, he made the more productive move of heading back to the shore and swinging by Salty Pete's to see if his family needed help cleaning up. Jace and Shelby were long gone—having departed even before Tanner, in a car tied with tin cans and draped with streamers, setting off for a hotel in Charleston for the night before leaving on a Caribbean honeymoon tomorrow. But Rick and Mia were still there, along with his parents, packing up decorations in boxes, and taking down the white arbor and chairs to be returned to a rental place.

"Think your girlfriend was mad you left, dude," Rick said to Tanner as he silently joined in folding up white wooden chairs in the now dusky beach air. The sun had just set, leaving behind electric streaks of pink in the western sky, lighting their work from the opposite side of the open-air building. Mia and their parents were cleaning up inside, leaving the two brothers in privacy.

"She's not my girlfriend," Tanner groused.

"Better tell *her* that," Rick advised him.

"I've tried, but I'm not sure she hears me." And it was all too apropos that just then his phone notified him that he'd been tagged in a picture on Facebook. He stopped what he was doing to look—and found Ashlynn had posted the selfie from earlier. Unbeknownst to him, she'd managed to get the bride and groom in the picture, in the distance, behind them. She'd captioned it: *I wonder who will be next? ;)* It made him grit his teeth.

For the first time since he'd arrived, Rick stopped what he was doing and shot him a glance. "Where'd you disappear to earlier anyway?"

He stuck his phone back in his pocket. "Had to look at a job."

"Where at?" Common enough question, especially in a small town.

"Rosebud," he said. Much less common answer—and Rick's eyes went wide.

"Josie's parents called *you* to do work for them?" The Bells and Roses had mostly avoided each other for the last seven years—somehow that seemed easier than pretending everything was okay.

Now he only wished that were the answer because it

would feel a hell of a lot simpler. "Not exactly. Josie's back. Moving into Rosebud. Called Ronnie Tucker but accidentally got me instead. We were both pretty shocked."

His brother appeared equally as dumbstruck. "You're kidding? She's back? Just like that?"

"Just like that." Not that Tanner even knew what that meant. After seven years of silence, it's not like she would suddenly reach out to let him know her plans. Their lives had been separate for a very long time now.

"You set her up with some other contractor then?"

He gave his head a slight shake. "No."

And even without looking at Rick, Tanner could almost feel his older brother's eyes flying wide. "No?" Then he drew back. "You're not working for her?"

"Said I would," he replied, keeping it simple as he added another folded white chair to a row of them resting against a railing.

But Rick had quit putting away chairs altogether. "What on earth are you thinking?"

That was actually a damn good question. He wasn't even sure how the conversation had gone from "you'd be a terrible innkeeper" to "let's build an amphitheater." He only knew it had been *his* stupid idea. Because he'd always thought she could make more of a career *here* if she wanted to—she'd just forever had her sights set solely on Nashville. And because— hell—even after everything, that quickly he'd felt drawn to her, drawn to helping her, drawn to making her happy. He hadn't *wanted* to feel that way, but old stuff between them— the good stuff—had somehow come rushing back under- neath all the negative emotion.

Now he wasn't sure he'd done the right thing. Maybe he should have just told her to go to hell. But instead— somehow—he'd promised to build her a stage. For free, more or less. What *had* he been thinking?

"Not sure," he finally told his brother.

Then Rick gave his head a pointed tilt and said, "You're not getting back together with her, are you?"

At this, Tanner's head shot up to meet his brother's gaze. "Hell no."

"Good," Rick said. "Because that would be crazy."

"I'm just doing a job here, that's all. It's all business." Okay, except the part about doing it pretty much for free. But Rick didn't need to know that part.

"I hope so. I mean, I don't even know why you're doing a project for her, bro—but my advice is to get in, and get back out. Work fast. And keep your contact with her to a minimum. She treated you like shit—and you don't need more of that."

"Of course I don't. But this has nothing to do with that— it's work, plain and simple." Even though it *was* a good reminder. Josie had always had a way of getting under his skin, and maybe that was what had happened this afternoon at Rosebud, that fast. He wouldn't let it happen again.

And in fact, maybe he *should* back out. She'd given him the easy out, after all. He'd made an impulsive offer—he'd be well within his rights to withdraw it.

But as dusk turned to dark and he started carrying chairs to Rick's truck, he decided that backing out would be like... holding a grudge. And following through would be...proving that nothing between them mattered anymore. It would be putting this, and her, behind him once and for all.

❧

WHEN JOSIE LAY down to sleep that night, in her old bed, in her old room, everything felt surreal. It was strange enough to be back at home—the sprawling house half-filled with furniture because her parents and left some behind—but having Tanner show up when she'd least expected it? It had put her brain—and her body—on overload.

She'd never stopped loving him. And she'd always known that—but if there was any question about it at all, it had been answered almost the second she'd laid eyes on him.

His departure had been nearly as awkward as his arrival. After adding gas to the tank of the truck he'd restored for her, he'd seemed to remember all the reasons he should be mad and had gone a bit brusque again. He'd stopped making eye contact and climbed in to his own pickup, saying wood-enly, "I'll be back in a few days."

She almost couldn't believe that he was going to build her a stage—and she still had no idea if it was a good idea or a crazy one. All she knew for certain was that she ached to see him again, that she was—this quickly—living for the moment he'd show back up at Rosebud.

This is not good, not good at all. It had taken every ounce of strength within her to drive away from him all those years ago, a move she'd felt she had to make to allow them both to follow the paths that called to them. But she'd not expected to come home and end up feeling desperately in need of him mere hours after her arrival.

Sleep was slow in coming, but when she opened her eyes the next morning—sun blazing in through the thinning pink-and-white polka dotted curtains of her girlhood—she felt…happy. Happier than she had in a very long time. Maybe happier than she'd really felt since driving away from Sassafras seven years ago.

Yesterday she'd been a puppy with its tail between its legs, crawling home broke and a failure. But today she felt…new hope. She truly did love this house. She truly did love Tanner. She wasn't sure what would happen now, but life suddenly seemed fresh and full of possibilities again in a way she couldn't have predicted twenty-four hours ago.

Tossing on well-worn blue jeans and a loose sweater, she walked down the quiet dirt lane to the faded blue Chevy, then drove two hours north up the coast past Charleston to Myrtle Beach. She called Daphne on the way and asked if her sister could meet her at their parents' new condo. She'd never actually been there before, but located the address easily. "Surprise!" she said when her mother opened the door. "I'm home!"

The truth was that it made her sad, seeing her mom and dad in a modern condo complex—it felt a world away from Rosebud and their quiet, rural Low Country home. And it was a somber reminder that life changed; people got older, time marched on, and sometimes things—and even whole ways of existence—got left behind. It was all the more impetus for what she was about to ask them.

Once Daphne arrived and she answered their questions with more of a "decided it wasn't working in Nashville and missed home" slant than an "I'm broke and desperate" one, she said, "And now I have a confession to make."

The truth was, she could make *lots* of confessions if she wanted to—about being broke and desperate, about how demoralizing her life in Music City had been, about disillusionment and injustices—but the current admission was more pressing. "I yanked the *For Sale* sign out of the yard and took the house off the market."

As their faces all fell in confusion, Daphne said, "But how could you do that? Your name wasn't on the contract."

Josie gritted her teeth in a eek-please-don't-kill me smile. "Remember how people used to mistake us for each other on the phone? They still do."

Daphne, however, did not look amused. "You impersonated me?"

Josie held up her hand, leaving a small space between index finger and thumb. "Just a little."

25

Her sister rolled her eyes. It wasn't the first time for that, and it probably wouldn't be the last—Daphne had been born with the practical gene Josie hadn't, and was among the multitudes that didn't always appreciate how Josie's mind worked.

"Sorry, Daph," Josie said. "It was an impulsive move—I should have come to you first."

Her sister just sighed—even if she didn't *get* Josie, she still loved her. "But why did you take the house off the market? I thought you needed the money from the sale." Their parents were financially comfortable, and the plan had been to split the proceeds from the house between the two sisters. For Josie, it would have been a windfall—enough to support her for several more years in Nashville or wherever else she wanted to live.

"I did," she explained, "but the house doesn't seem to be drawing any buyers and it's starting to look a little rundown in the meantime. So..." She stopped, took a deep breath for what was coming. "I want to move home for good and live in Rosebud. And..." She looked to her sister. "I know that's not fair—that fifty percent of it is yours—but once I figure out how to make some money, I can start paying you for your half. Like maybe monthly installments or something?" she suggested hopefully. "And there's more."

Daphne was straight-faced, her voice dry. "I can't wait."

Josie held up her hands. "Now bear with me for this next part. I...want to build a stage and some seating on the grounds, and sing there, and host other musicians, and maybe rent it out as a general event space."

At this, neither Daphne or her parents' faces changed at all—frozen by the strange new idea—and they all stayed quiet.

"I know what you're thinking," Josie went on. "This is just another one of Josie's crazy, impulsive ideas. But here's the kicker. It wasn't my idea at all. It was Tanner's." She smiled, hoping they would see that this fact instantly made it a more sensible concept.

Even though they all said *"Tanner's?"* in unison and utter shock.

But she stuck to the main topic. "And Tanner is smart. And not impulsive at all. So if it's his idea, that probably means it's a good one. And if I can't sing at the Grand Ole Opry, well, at least I can still sing *somewhere*—and that...well, that makes everything feel a little bit better to me. Just knowing I can sing someplace, for somebody. Even if it's just a few people. That would be enough to...you know...keep me from feeling dead inside."

Again, they just stared at her, clearly dumbstruck. And okay, she'd gotten a little heavy there. But it was the truth. She hadn't gone to Nashville and left the love of her life for fun and games—she'd done it because singing and playing her guitar was the fuel her soul needed, and without it she'd feared her heart would wither away to nothing.

She was wondering if she should go on trying to convince them when Daphne murmured, "Wow. I had no idea."

"No idea what?" Josie asked.

"Well...that not singing would make you feel *that* bad."

"It's...like breathing to me," she explained simply.

And then Daphne surprised her, reaching out to take her hand. She spoke quietly. "If this is what you need, Josie, then yes, it's okay."

And Josie could see in her older sister's eyes how much she'd just felt Josie's words—and that maybe it was the first time she'd ever really understood just how much a part of Josie her music was. Maybe it took growing up, adulthood, to really start understanding some things. Still, it caught her off-guard, and she whispered, "Really?"

Daphne nodded. "Really."

Josie drew in a big breath, blew it back out. Surprise. Relief. "Thank you. Thank you so much. And I'll pay you back as quickly as I can, I promise!"

Yet Daphne shook her head. "It doesn't matter." She and her husband, Mitch, were also fine financially, pulling down well over six figures a year.

Yet Josie insisted, "It *does* matter. To me." She squeezed her sister's hand.

Next, of course, her family wanted to know how on earth she'd gotten back in touch with Tanner so quickly and why he was doing this for her. She filled them in, concluding with, "I don't really know why, but I'm grateful to have the help on a new start that means something to me."

Though as she climbed back into the Chevy pickup after an impromptu lunch on her parents' shiny new condo balcony, she began to wonder exactly what she was getting herself into here. She had to pay Tanner back for an amphitheater. And now she had to pay her sister back for half a house. And she had no income to speak of. Maybe this was just another Josie pie-in-the-sky plan, more Josie in-the-moment thinking and wishing and hoping—maybe when all was said and done, she was going to end up worse off than when she'd come rolling back into Sassafras yesterday morning.

Jump and the net will appear. She used to believe that. And so she'd jumped. She'd jumped all the way to Tennessee and Music Row. But no net had caught her there. So she'd come home thinking Rosebud was...well, a surer, safer net to catch her. Because it was home. It had felt like a sound, safe, practical decision.

And yet, despite that sane, sensible turn toward practicality, here she was—jumping again. Because...Tanner. His idea. His sweat and blood and creativity going into it. And it all sounded amazing and beautiful. She was jumping because she still loved the man who believed it was a good endeavor. And because she so badly wanted to keep making music.

Please let there be a net this time. Please let there be a net.

CHAPTER FOUR

*J*osie's parents had forced her to take a check for five hundred dollars. She'd hated taking it, but the truth was that she needed groceries, and would have utility bills and other typical homeowning expenses now. So—despite the fact that it would have felt easier to just hibernate for a while at Rosebud rather than risk facing more people in town who knew what she'd done to Tanner—she drove straight into Sassafras, pulled to the curb on Main Street, and walked into the Sassafras Deposit Bank.

As she got out of the truck, she felt a little like a teenager opening a first checking account—but these were the steps a person had to take to get reestablished in life. *Note to self: Add Mom and Dad to the list of people you owe money to.*

As she approached a teller's window in the old bank building, the woman on the other side said, "Josie Bell? Is that you?"

She braced herself. "Susan McBeal?" She remembered her old classmate as sort of a judgmental busybody. Who would likely ask her a bunch of personal questions. "Yep, it's me."

"Well, this is a surprise. What can I do for you today?"

"I, uh, need to open a checking account." Josie sucked in her breath, a little embarrassed—mostly because Susan would see the check made out to her and know the account consisted solely of money from her parents. Hence feeling like a teenager—and an unenterprising one at that.

"Really? Does this mean you're home to stay?"

"Yes—I'm moving back into Rosebud."

She waited for the inevitable. *Couldn't hack it in Nashville? Can't afford your own place? Mom and Dad helping you out?* And maybe she'd top it off with, *You should be run out of town on a rail for what you did to Tanner Rose.* But as Susan took the endorsed check and typed some information into a computer, she only said, "Well, welcome back to Sassafras. You gonna be doing any singing anywhere? I always did like your voice."

All the tension in Josie's body relaxed. Okay, maybe Susan was nicer than she remembered. Or maybe she'd just grown up—like Daphne, like Tanner, like most everyone did. "I'm... actually working on that. I'll keep you posted."

Susan smiled. "Please do. I'll bring my husband and some friends out to see you—we love good country music."

Exiting the bank onto Main still sighing with relief, and imbued with fresh courage, she looked up and down the old-fashioned small town street at the businesses, wondering if any of them were hiring. Who knew—maybe her soon-to-be music venue would solve all of her financial woes, but for now, she needed to start bringing in some money, even if it was only a little.

The first thing her eyes fell on was the sign for the Rose Tavern, but she quickly x-ed it off the list of potential places of employment—Rick Rose surely hated her for the way she'd left Tanner. And Tanner's oldest brother had always intimidated her a little anyway. But she started hitting up other businesses, one after the other.

On the downside, she discovered that no help was needed at the hardware store, drug store, or deli. On the upside, Tom Coplan—who'd owned the hardware store her whole life—recognized her, welcomed her home, and asked her to tell her parents hello. And Ida Mae at the deli also seemed pleased to see her, was polite as everyone else in not asking what had brought her home from Nashville, and informed her that Delia's Grocery out near the shore was looking for a part-time cashier.

An hour later, she had a job with Delia, a forty-some-thing woman she'd known her whole life and who also seemed happy to see her back in town. She'd learned that Delia, who mostly ran the small store outside town by herself, wanted to have a little more time with her aging parents. And though Josie's parents weren't as old at Delia's, she understood where the other woman was coming from. Even being two hours away, she'd get to see a lot more of her family than she had these past years when she'd barely had enough money to make it home at Christmas for a few days.

"Now it's only minimum wage, Josie," Delia cautioned her, leaving Josie to suspect it had been intended as more of an after-school job for a teenager than for someone who needed an actual income.

But Josie assured her, "I'll take whatever I can get—just need a little cash coming in while I get settled." A small paycheck while she waited—hoped—for her net.

~

SHE SPENT the next few days cleaning and organizing the sprawling house, as well as working her first couple of shifts at Delia's, and buying some groceries for herself while she was there.

Of course, Tanner stayed on her mind the whole time. And the ache for him in her bones continued. It had never really gone away, but Lord knew that seeing him again so unexpectedly had brought back her desire with the force of thousand amplifiers.

She began to wonder in certain lonely moments if maybe he'd come to his senses, changed his mind, and wouldn't ever show back up. Or...maybe she'd dreamed the whole thing. It had certainly *seemed* like a dream.

But on the fourth day, as she knelt in the front yard weeding some overgrown perennial beds her father had planted when she was in high school, she heard the approach of a vehicle and looked up to see her old love behind the wheel.

Her heart lurched and she pushed to her feet, brushing loose soil from the thighs of the old torn and tattered blue jeans she wore. Could he see her emotions? She tried like hell to hide them as she walked to the gate and gave her best casual, "Hey."

"Hey." Spoken dryly, like at the beginning of their last encounter. But at least he'd returned.

"You're back." She hadn't quite meant to say that, but the words spilled out anyway.

"Said I would be. Want to look at the plans I drew up?"

She nodded, attempting not to appear overly enthusiastic as she exited the gate, watching as he unfolded some sheets of paper on the hood of his truck.

What she saw there instantly made her heart sing. The wide, octagonal stage reverberated with simple yet rich character, even just in the drawing. "There'll be an awning to protect performers from the weather if needed," he said, "and it'll extend in the rear to a small backstage sort of area. The

33

benches will be simple, rustic—logs sawn in half and sanded down, then varnished to make them hold up."

He went on to explain, "I want to make it all blend in with the landscape as much as possible. We'll leave as many trees and other greenery as we can, and that'll be easy since most of the work can be done without bringing in heavy equipment." He pointed back to his drawings. "We'll pour the steps leading down, but I'm keeping concrete to a minimum—we'll use mulch and other natural materials on pathways as needed. And I want to leave as much grass as we can, and if foot traffic wears it down too badly, we'll cross that bridge then. I'm thinking once the stage is in place, you might want to plant some wisteria or clematis around it—let it vine up onto the awning and make the stage feel that much more a part of the landscape."

"Or...roses," she added gently. "Pink."

And he immediately said, a bit more softly, "Of course. Pink roses. That...makes sense."

Although the grounds sported many kinds of flowers, pink rose bushes dotted the yard, and pink climbing roses ascended a trellis alongside the house and an arbor in back. They had presumably given the house its name—or maybe it was the other way around, no one was sure—but pink roses were as much a part of Rosebud as the home itself. And as luck would have it, pink roses had always been Josie's favorite—so much that she'd carried them to their senior prom, and Tanner had given her a single pink rose on the night he'd proposed to her.

Was he remembering that night right now, like she was? Was he remembering the way they'd made love in the grass after she'd said yes. He'd asked her in the front yard, mere steps from where they now stood. "I wanted to wait, Jos— wanted to take you out, wine and dine you, make it special— but damn, you look so pretty, and I'm kinda nervous, and I just need to do this now." Then he'd dropped to one knee on the front stone walkway and pulled out a ring.

"This *is* special," she'd assured him. "*Everything* with you is special."

No one had been home, and they'd fallen to the cool evening lawn kissing, touching, and one thing had led to another. Afterward, they'd lie on their backs looking up at the stars, and she'd found the pink rose that he'd dropped in the heat of passion and clutched it to her chest, experiencing the most perfect joy she could have imagined.

Hard to believe she'd given that up.

And now, her heart beat like a drum. She didn't know if it was because she was so excited about the plans for Rosebud's future or due to standing so close to Tanner, remembering that pink rose and that night in the grass—but she was pretty sure it was the latter. He smelled musky and masculine and downright hot.

Trying her damnedest to focus on the outdoor theater plans, she said, "I love it. I absolutely love it, Tanner."

But when she dared shift her gaze from the hood of the truck up to his blue, blue eyes, her skin rippled with desire and the juncture of her thighs fluttered with good old-fashioned want. She hadn't realized it until this moment, but she hadn't felt this in seven long years. Sure, she'd dated other guys, and she'd thought she'd experienced the flare of longing for a man, but it was nothing compared to this, a hunger that was pure and deep, and as hot as Sassafras on a steamy summer night.

The power of her reaction made her lower her chin, bite her lip. But she never took her eyes from his—couldn't, in fact—and suspected everything she felt was wafting from her skin like heat from fresh-laid asphalt on a sun-beaten South Carolina day.

His gaze locked on hers, and she knew—without doubt—

he felt it too. The heat between them hadn't faded, for him either.

She wanted to touch him so badly she could taste it. Wanted to kiss him. Drown in him. Let every sensation he brought out in her swallow her, own her. Would he touch her? Should *she* touch *him*? Or maybe it wasn't a question of should or shouldn't—but more one of how much longer could she keep *from* it?

That was when he took a step back. Lowered his eyes. "Glad you like it, but I gotta go."

"Oh." It came out, a surprised murmur, as she tried to get hold of herself and come back to planet Earth. Where they were no longer a couple. Where she was just lucky he didn't hate her guts. "Okay." She took a small step back, too.

He ceased to look at her again, instead busying himself with gathering up his papers from on top of the truck, folding them haphazardly and shoving them into a brown flip-top folder. "If it's okay with you, I'll get started day after tomorrow."

"Just you? No crew?" Oh crap. Did she sound too happy about that?

He blinked uncertainly, starting toward the driver's side door. "Some of it I'll need help on and bring a few guys in when they're off other projects, but a lot of it I can handle on my own."

"Okay. Cool." Trying to sound casual again. As if it didn't matter at all. But inside she remained delighted that he was planning to do this job himself. Because it meant he cared. He wanted to be here. Same as *she* wanted him here. Even if he was backing away right now.

"I, um, may or may not be here when you get started," she informed him. "I got part-time work at Delias's."

This brought his eyes back to hers. "That's good," was all he said, but his voice held more—he was impressed and maybe a little surprised that she'd taken even that one small practical step. And she felt good about it, too. *I can change. I can balance practicality with dreams.*

"Or…maybe I *will* be," she offered up then, "since it's only a few days a week." *Maybe I'll get to see you some more, talk to you some more, watch you working in the hot sun, watch you helping me rebuild my life.*

"Doesn't matter," he said.

"No," she agreed, lying.

"Gotta go," he said again.

She just nodded. But as he got in and slammed the door, she found herself approaching the open window. Because she owed him…well, a lot, but at the moment, gratitude took the lead. "Tanner," she said, "thank you. So, so much."

He just shrugged. Started the engine. "Take care, Josie."

She backed away, watching from near the gate as he turned around and departed, leaving a trail of dust in his wake.

Her heart still beat too fast as she let herself back in the yard. And her mind spun. Memories of pink roses and engagement rings and hot sex on the ground pummeled her. Kisses by bonfires. And Christmas trees. On summer nights. And winter ones, too. They'd given each other their virginity in the backseat of his first car, an old Mustang he'd bought with money earned working for his parents at their family-run garden center.

But stop thinking so much. About the past. The future. What did *happen. What* could *happen. Just get back to work.*

Yes, that was a good idea. She dropped back to her knees and picked up the trowel and resumed digging in the dirt.

It didn't matter if there was still heat between them, since he obviously didn't want to act on it. And who could blame him? She really needed to just get grounded here—be thankful he was doing this project for her and grateful for the new hope it had given her. And that was all. Because nothing else was going to happen. It would be a terrible idea anyway. There was just too much history—too much that she knew he could never forgive. Memories were nice. But that was all they were—memories.

When the sound of an approaching vehicle shook her from her thoughts, she again pushed to her feet, trowel in hand—surprised to spot Tanner's truck rambling back up the lane. He'd come back.

Had he forgotten to discuss something with her about the amphitheater?

Before she could even move from where she stood, though, he'd slammed his truck door and come marching through the gate, practically flinging it open. The expression on his face was one of anger as he strode briskly toward her. Her whole body tensed as she murmured, "What?"

His eyes glimmered darkly on her despite the brightness of the day, and he muttered, "Damn it, Josie," just before he bracketed her face with his hands and kissed her.

CHAPTER FIVE

*P*art of Tanner knew this was madness—but a bigger part of him just didn't care. A bigger part of him had simply succumbed to following the instincts and urges and compulsions inside him. As he'd driven away, every molecule of his body had pulsed with longing for her. The molecules between his legs most of all—somehow just standing near her had turned him hard as a board.

And he'd found himself turning the truck around. Barreling back toward her. Like a damn madman. A man with no control over his actions. And he still didn't have any because he was kissing her like there was no tomorrow—and no surrender had ever felt better.

She kissed him back—he'd known she would. He'd felt the desire dripping from her same as it was from him. It was hard to believe he still wanted her like that after the way things had ended between them—but he wasn't going to think about that right now. Right now was only about pleasure.

One hot kiss turned into another, and another. And he wasn't sure whose hands moved first, to undressing the other

—he only knew he was pulling the t-shirt off over her head to find a baby blue bra underneath and that her fingers were at his belt, then his zipper.

To see her like this again, now, felt unreal. Her petite body had been perfect to him then—and it was still that way now. As her bra came off, his hands went instantly to her round breasts, tipped in dark, dusky pink, and a hot cry of pleasure left her as his mouth closed over her there. Her fingers threaded through his hair and soon they dropped together to their knees. The scents of earth and spring roses filled his senses, somehow fueling his need to be inside her. It had been too long. Way too long.

Neither of them spoke. There were a million words that wanted to spill from him, but he held each one in—because it was all too damn complicated. And this—this mutual hunger between them—was maybe the one thing that was simple here. They both felt it. Always had. And always would, it seemed.

But when she touched him where he was hard for her, it felt like...history. A safe place and a wickedly dangerous destination all at once. She was the first woman to ever touch him that way, the first he'd ever taken to bed—hell, the first girl he'd kissed. So...maybe even this part wasn't so simple after all—but it felt too damn good, and too damn powerful, to even think about stopping.

They both kicked their shoes off, shoved their jeans to the ground. He laid her back on the carpet of grass beneath the Spanish moss, parted her legs, and pushed his way deep inside. Low groans left them both. It was coming home. For both of them. In a far different way than she'd come home to Rosebud. This went soul deep.

She whispered his name and he rasped hers in return. She clung to his neck as he moved inside her, thrusting hard and deep—again, again, again—giving himself over to the untamed urges she inspired. He closed his eyes—partly trying to hold back a little, and partly trying to make this... something different than it was. Maybe he was trying to forget who he was with, what that meant. Trying to make it just sex, lust, nothing more. But there was no shutting out the scents and sounds and feel of her—even with eyes shut tight, everything was Josie. Her touch on his skin, the way her legs wrapped around him, the hot, sweet sighs that echoed from her lips—he could never have mistaken her for any other woman.

They rolled on the lawn until she was astride him— grinding, riding him, her eyes shut as well now, head tipped back in pleasure. He kneaded her breasts and watched her face, felt her beauty, hated her for leaving him, loved her for coming back.

Are you trying to forget this is me underneath you right now? If she was, he knew in his soul that she wasn't succeeding any more than he had.

But soon he forgot to think about that. Soon he was too caught up in the hot beauty of her moving on him, chasing her passion as hard as she'd ever chased anything else, including her dreams. At one point, she bent forward, lowering her beautiful pale breasts, tipped in pink, toward his mouth until one nipple was inside. He latched on, suckled her. Went all the more rigid between his legs for the added sensation, thrust up into her harder.

It had, once upon a time, been their thing. Suckling her breasts while she leaned over him that way had always been one of the things that took her that last little distance, pushed her over the edge, made her come. Some things never changed, he supposed—and this, now, forced him to feel their past all the more intensely.

He drove up into her, suckling hard at one turgid nipple, until she cried out in climax, holding nothing back—and mere seconds later he came, too, teeth clenched in the dark pleasure of it.

And then...sanity. Or was that *in*sanity? That moment you realize what a stupid thing you've just done. Because perfect or not—nope, this wasn't simple at all. It made something that was already a mess a hell of a lot messier.

She rolled off him, over onto her back, so they lay side by side in the grass.

"Almost the very same spot," she said softly.

He didn't have to ask what she meant. "Yep." The same thing had happened right here on the night he'd asked her to marry him. At the moment, though, that proposal felt like a pretty big joke and like he was a pretty big fool.

It made him not want to be here anymore. So he sat up, glanced around for his pants—reached for them.

That was when her hand clamped down on his wrist. "No."

He looked at her. "What?"

"No, you can't go. Not yet. Not fair."

He narrowed his gaze on her. "You're a fine one to talk about what's fair."

She pursed her lips, clearly tried to hide that it stung—but he didn't care. Still, she said, "We just had sex, Tanner. You can't just leave. We need to talk. About a lot of things."

He drew in his breath, knowing what she was asking was perfectly reasonable. Even if the last thing he wanted to do was talk. "Fine," he bit off. "But I'm putting my pants on first."

They both dressed and, standing up, she took his hand and led him to an old hammock hung between two trees. They'd made out in it as teenagers. Damn, everything here was a memory.

Wordlessly, they lay down together, his arm coming around her as the fabric cocooned them, her head on his shoulder and her palm pressed to his chest through his tee.

After a moment of silence that started to feel a little too comfortable—because he didn't *want* things getting comfortable here, because he was still pissed as hell—he said what came to mind. "I don't even know you anymore, Josie. I don't know anything about you."

Next to him, she sighed. "Yes you do. Believe it or not, not much has changed. All in all, I'm just a little more world-weary."

"So tell me about Nashville," he invited her. "Tell me about the last seven years."

Another sigh. "Let's see. I held waitressing jobs. Shared rundown apartments with strangers. I made demos, and sang in bars, and went on auditions. Some of the auditions seemed promising but didn't pan out. Other times they told me my sound was too old-fashioned or that I have too much twang in my voice—one guy said, 'Tammy Wynette is dead, honey.'"

To Tanner, Josie's sound had always been the purest sort of country music, and he thought it was a shame if that was no longer in style. "I always *liked* the twang in your voice," he confessed softly.

"I signed with a music publisher for a little while," she went on, "to let him try to sell some of my songs—but nothing ever came of it. And I also met men who...who, well, promised to make me a star, for a price."

At this, Tanner drew back slightly to look at her. "Like, sex?"

"Yeah," she said sadly. "And of course I ran screaming in the other direction each time, but it was still horrible and offensive and dirty and made me feel like crap."

"Each time. So it happened that way more than once?"

She nodded against his shoulder. "So often that...well, until recently I'd almost forgotten some guys are nice."

Something primal in him wanted to pound every entitled,

43

disrespectful, manipulative asshole who'd ever dared bother her into the ground—but he fought down the urge, remembering that it had been a long time since she'd been his to fight for. Even so, he said, "I'm sorry that happened, Jos. I might be mad as hell at you, but no woman deserves that."

"The last time it happened, with a producer I really thought was really a nice guy, interested in my music—well, I guess it just did me in. Made me tired of trying. Tired of living in poverty chasing a dream that might never come true. Right after that, I got fired from my last waitressing job —when an obnoxious customer complained about my service after I refused to let him grope me—and it almost felt like a sign. When I couldn't even pay my measly part of the rent last week, I...well, I didn't even feel like I had a choice anymore."

"You could have sold the truck," he told her. Had she never thought of that? "Would probably bring a decent price."

She gasped in response, catching him off-guard—then lifted her head to look down at him and say, "I would never sell the truck, Tanner. Ever."

"Why not?"

"I love it. And it's from you."

That pulled at his heartstrings—even as it rankled something inside him. "If I mean so damn much to you, Josie, why'd you leave that way?" Shit, he hadn't quite meant to throw it out there so plainly, but too late.

She shut her eyes for a second, looking pained, then reopened them. "Because we wanted two different things, Tanner. And you got to have yours, here. But I didn't. And I didn't want to wake up one day when I was eighty wondering...could I have done it? Could I have made it? Could I have been a big star? It haunted me. And I loved you—I loved you like crazy—but even though you supported my music in

44

general, I didn't feel like you really understood just how much it meant to me. Like you just wanted me to see it as a nice hobby and get down to the business of making myself content here." Then her brow knit slightly. "And thing is— now...I think I am. I came home because I was broke, but I think I really actually want to be here, that I appreciate Sassafras more than I used to. And Rosebud. And my family. But back then...well—I just had to try.

"And no words can ever make up for it, I know—I went about it all wrong. But I thought if I told you, you'd just talk me out of it, or act like I was being crazy, or impulsive, or—"

"Wait," he interrupted her. "That's not me. I never came down on you for being impulsive—that was everybody else."

She nodded. "Fair enough. And one of the reasons I loved you. But you would have tried to convince me it was a wacky thing to do. And I just kept envisioning this big, horrible scene where we're both crying and begging each other to do what the other one wants. And I thought—why put us through that? It was a weak decision, I know. But I just couldn't bear seeing you hurt. So I took the coward's way out. And you may not believe me or ever truly understand this, but driving away from you was the hardest thing I ever had to do, the worst thing I ever did. And...my biggest regret."

Tanner took all that in. She was right. He couldn't understand it. Even if he tried. And hell—his heart was bending in his chest, with everything he still felt for her, everything seven years hadn't taken away...but how could he ever trust her again? He couldn't. And that made all of this seem, well... irrelevant. Maybe good to clear the air, but he didn't feel any less hurt than he had back then.

Just then, his phone buzzed from his pocket.

And rather than come up with some sort of reply to everything she'd just said, it seemed easier to reach for the phone. Ashlynn's name appeared on the screen—a missed call. What timing.

"Oh God, are you, like, married or anything?" Josie asked in a rush. She'd seen the name, too, even though he'd darkened the screen as quickly as he could. "I mean, I didn't even ask you anything about your life now."

"Hell no, I'm not married," he informed her brusquely, a little offended. "If I were married, I sure as hell wouldn't be here right now."

Next to him, she let out a big sigh of relief. "You're right. I know. Like I said, sometimes I think I've forgotten what an honorable man is like. I've dealt with too many snakes in the grass."

Yet then her gaze narrowed on him suspiciously—maybe he looked guilty. "You have a girlfriend, though, don't you?"

He took a second forming an answer. "Not...officially."

"Officially?"

"I've been seeing this girl awhile—and she's more into it than I am. But we never officially made it exclusive."

"Though she probably thinks it is, right?"

He shrugged. "I'm...not sure."

She sighed. "Yes you are. She thinks she's your girlfriend. Which turns me into...yuck...someone I don't want to be. Blegh."

"You didn't do anything wrong," he told her. "Well, other than leaving me high and dry seven years ago. But you didn't do anything wrong *today*."

"Thanks. I think." Then a cute, easy, distant sort of smile made its way onto her face as she peered up through the limbs hung with Spanish moss above them. It was an easy Josie smile he remembered all too well.

"What are you smiling about?" he asked. But he was pretty sure he already knew. Since some things never changed.

"I just got a tune in my head."

Yep, just like old times. Songs would come to her randomly and she'd tell him. Sing what was coming together in her mind. She did the same now.

"I'd never sell the truck that you gave me,

It's the only thing I have left from you.

I'd never sell the truck, even when I'm down on my luck,

It's the memory of a love that was true."

Despite himself, despite the line about true love, he laughed. "I'm not sure that's your best, Jos."

She just shrugged, grinned, looking pretty as sin. "It's a work in progress. And a country song. Where beauty is in the eye of the beholder. One man's trash…"

"Listen," he said. "I'm sorry you didn't make it in Nashville. And, even if it messed up my life some, I admire you for going after what you wanted. And sticking with it this long. At least you gave it your all."

She nodded, smiled a small smile, even if she looked a little sad. "Yeah, at least I won't grow old wondering now. And I can get my life on track here."

After that, they caught up on other things. She asked about his family and he informed her Jace had just gotten married and Rick would do the same in a couple of months. He told her how the three brothers had invested together in a race car that Jace was driving on dirt tracks around the region. And that their parents had retired from the garden center they'd run for Josie's whole life, turning it over to Jace.

When he inquired about hers, he found out her dad had retired as well, early, from the sheet metal business he'd started with his brother when they were young, and that her parents moved to Myrtle Beach to be near her sister.

"I'm surprised they'd let go of this place," he said. "After it being in the family for generations."

"I was, too. Even if it's more house than anyone really

needs these days and was a lot to take care of. It's not why I came home, but being able to keep it in the family is a definite perk. I guess I didn't I realize how much I cared about Rosebud until now."

"So your mom and dad didn't need to sell to get the condo?" he asked.

She shook her head. "He sold his half of the business when he retired and it created a nice nest egg. They're comfortable financially." Then went on to share, "If they or Daphne had known how destitute I was in Nashville, I'm sure they'd have sent me money—but I didn't want that. I didn't want to be the adult child who sponges off her parents. It sucks bad enough that I'm the adult child who hasn't made anything of herself and is getting deeper in debt by the day. So I made out to them like things were more comfortable than they really were."

She went on to tell him a bit about her parents' new place, and about Daphne's life—she'd married Mitch, a beach resort mogul, five years ago and they were busy trying to get pregnant. He filled her in on his brother's significant others as well, both of whom he liked.

"Lots of changes all around," she mused.

And something about the way she said it made him feel… well, like he needed to protect himself here. Make things clear. In case she was hinting that things could change between *them*, too.

"Listen, Josie," he began. "What just happened between us here…"

"Yeah?"

"It can't happen again."

Her face fell a bit, even if she tried not to let it show. "Because of the girlfriend who isn't a girlfriend but really *is* a girlfriend."

"No, that's not it," he assured her. "It's because…we're

over. You made that choice a long time ago. And I worked too hard to get over you to go back there again. Surely you understand that."

She pursed her lips, hesitated, nodded. "Okay."

"And I'm happy to build this stage for you, and hope it might get you on your feet again, but...it's a favor from an old friend, for old time's sake. That's all it *can* be."

"Okay," she said again.

"And...I should go." *Because things are getting awkward again. Because I made them that way. But I had to make my position crystal clear.*

"Sure," she said quietly.

He rolled out of the hammock onto his feet, then held out a hand to help her up.

Yet she said, "No, I think I'll just lie here awhile."

"All right." He nodded. "I'll be back to get started on the stage in a couple of days. Bye, Josie."

"Bye." Her voice stayed sad, resigned.

And he made a beeline for the gate. This never should have happened, but now he needed to put it behind him.

"Tanner," she called then.

He stopped, hand on the gate latch, and looked back across the yard.

"Just for the record, *I* never got over *you*."

The words settled heavy in his chest. But rather than reply, he pushed through the gate, ready to put that little bombshell behind him as well.

CHAPTER SIX

*W*ell, damn. Now he had to stop seeing Ashlynn. But if he cared so little about her that he'd just had sex with Josie without giving her a second thought, it was probably time. Hell, maybe it had been time months ago. She'd always wanted more than he did—and now, well, now he was remembering what it was like to have those kinds of gnawing, needful feelings.

He lay on his back in his kitchen, his head up under the sink inside a cabinet, installing a garbage disposal. He'd bought the rundown little brick ranch near town with the plan of flipping it, but had found out that when he worked on other people's projects all day, he wasn't motivated to work on his own at night. This was, in fact, the first home fix-up chore he'd done in months—motivated by needing the distraction.

But so far, it wasn't helping much. Two women plagued his thoughts, even with his back aching from the awkward position and his focus on tightening bolts. Ironically, though, he'd be breaking up with Ashlynn only to *not* keep seeing

Josie. Because he couldn't. Wouldn't. He was glad he'd been upfront with her about that.

Even if her last words kept haunting him. *I never got over you.*

Just like the rest of it, putting that out of his mind was easier said than done.

He still couldn't believe he'd gone back, still couldn't believe he'd had sex with her in the grass. But it was just a last hurrah. Taking care of unfinished business. That was all. Because when she'd left him all those years ago, in addition to breaking him emotionally, the truth was, he'd missed sex with her as much as any other part of their relationship. They'd always had a wild, potent chemistry that—if he was honest with himself—he'd yet to experience with anyone else. And what had happened yesterday proved it was still there, alive and well. But maybe being with her that way one last time would finally get it out of his system.

Yeah, that's why you're still thinking about it constantly over twenty-four hours later.

When you're not trying to figure out how to call it quits with Ashlynn.

Every time he envisioned telling Ashlynn, it almost made him ill. She would be crushed. And she was a nice girl—he'd never intended to hurt her, but he'd been careless with her feelings and now there was no avoiding it.

Much as he hated admitting it to himself, he was starting to understand—at least a little—why Josie had taken the easy way out. It wasn't fun to break somebody's heart.

But he couldn't get in a truck and leave—Ashlynn lived right over in Edisto Beach. Like it or not, he was going to have to face this. And hell, maybe facing it more maturely than Josie had would make it a little easier to walk away from *her.* It would remind him that he was at least doing the right thing, ending a relationship the right way. Even if the very idea nearly made him break out in hives.

Just then his phone rang—where he'd left it up above him on the kitchen counter.

He sat up and banged his head into the brand new garbage disposal. "Damn it," he groused—then maneuvered out from under the sink. He pressed one hand to the spot on his forehead now radiating pain, and with the other he reached up to grab the phone. It was Ashlynn. He didn't want to answer. But he did.

"Hey there," she said in her merry, cutesy way.

"Hey."

"You sound in a bad mood. Something wrong?"

"Just banged my head under the sink is all."

"Aw, ouch. Want me to come kiss it and make it better?"

He let out a sigh. "Ashlynn, we need to talk."

"About what?"

Shit, he should have thought this through a little better. Was it worse to make her wonder by saying what he just had on the phone, or worse if he'd just shown up at her place and dropped it on her like a bomb? Breaking up with someone wasn't in his wheelhouse. "You busy right now?"

"Not really. Just getting ready to paint my nails."

"Okay—I'm coming over." Again, maybe he should take a little time, prepare what he was going to say. But he was suddenly itching to barrel forward and get this done.

On the other end of the line, she giggled. "Is this, like, a booty call, Tanner?"

He blew out a tired sigh, his head still aching. "Not exactly."

~

DESPITE HERSELF, Josie was happy. Crazy happy. It didn't make sense at all—given that Tanner had been unequivocally clear that it was a one-time thing, and that he was still angry with her. Yet as she flitted merrily around the house, singing to herself, she remembered something Daphne had once told her. "When you're in love, even if the other person doesn't feel the same way, there's still a part of you that's happy, because love makes you that way."

So that must be it. Even Tanner's rejection couldn't quite ruin the elation of love. And how amazing it had been to be with him again that way. Just like on the night he'd proposed, it wasn't wine and candles, but the heat they generated together was palpable. And every sensation she'd experienced with him the other day continued to play through her mind, over and over.

Without quite meaning to, she started piecing together an up-tempo tune in her head, singing out loud as she got ready for a shift at the grocery store.

"Pink roses on the trellis,
Pink roses on the vine,
Pink roses in the bottle that held our favorite wine.
Pink roses pressed in pages,
A love story so fine,
Pink roses from the days when you were mine."

She pressed the audio record button on her phone and kept singing so she'd have a record of it for later.

Then she wrote a note, and on the way out, taped it to the gate.

I'M at Delia's if you need me for anything. Left house unlocked if you need to use the bathroom. Soda and water in the fridge—help yourself. Thank you again! xx oo

PART of her was sorry she wouldn't be there when he started work today. But another part of her—pushing the elation of love aside—figured maybe it was for the best. Since, again, he'd made his position clear. And if she couldn't have him, maybe it was better not to have him within arm's reach but still completely out of her grasp.

If she was here when he showed up, she'd probably act like a teenager and try to hang around him or watch him work or keep offering him snacks and drinks. So maybe being at Delia's allowed her to…well, start rebuilding that emotional distance a bit. At the very least, it kept her from behaving like a lovesick fool.

～

IT WAS a relief to Tanner that she wasn't there. Just took any temptation out of the equation—even if five little words kept sounding in his head even now. *I never got over you.*

But he kept trying like hell to quit hearing them as he got a good, solid start on the project. He dug post holes, sunk some pipe in them, poured some footers. He didn't need the drinks she offered—he carried his own in a cooler—but he did use the bathroom a couple times. Though he'd have to reprimand her about that note. *Josie, Josie, Josie*—some things never changed.

She wasn't there the next day, either, but his morning started with another handwritten message on the gate:

AT DELIA'S AGAIN TODAY. But I walked down last night to look at the work. I'm so excited to see it come together! I think I'm going to call it The Rosebud Stage. Or The Stage at Rosebud. Or the Rosebud Theater. Do any of those sound right to you? House is open—take whatever you like from the fridge. Thank you again, Tanner! xx oo

WHAT WAS it with the x's and o's? He didn't need to be thinking about her giving him any more kisses. But then, that was how Josie had always signed things when they were young, and again, apparently some things never changed.

It was a long day full of good work. He'd had some lumber dropped off at the top of the hill and toted it down, then spent the day building the stage floor, which would float above the ground and circumvented the need for Bobcat digging or laying a foundation all the way around. It would be a little less permanent that way if she ever wanted to take it out—or it could be reinforced later if that proved necessary.

By the end of the day, he began to feel...well, excited for her. Like his vision made sense and this place really was going to take off.

Not that he knew why he was doing something this nice for her. He kept telling his brother and her and himself that he was still angry with her—and he was—and yet he still wanted good things for her. She'd done wrong by him, but that didn't make her a bad person.

In fact, she was the sort of girl—woman now, definitely a woman—who spread a lot of light and cheer wherever she went. She made the world a happier place. Through her music, through her smile, through her live-in-the-moment attitude. Really, the most surprising thing to him after her leaving here was that she *hadn't* made it big, that some Nashville record bigwig hadn't seen the same light in her as he did and put it on display for the whole world to see.

Maybe that was why he was doing this. Because no

matter what she'd done to him, maybe he still thought her light should shine—somewhere, somehow.

And given that he'd pretty much snuffed out Ashlynn's light completely the other night, well...at least he could keep someone else's gleaming. She hadn't taken it well—he'd expected the tears, but not the begging. And the simply not being able to accept it. "I just don't understand why—I just need you to make me understand."

Because hot sex with my ex made me realize I don't feel anything for you at all. He'd not had the heart to say that, though, and he'd just stuck with it being time to move on and them wanting different things and him deciding he never wanted to get married or have kids. That last part was a blatant lie, but he'd been desperate at that point to convince her they didn't belong together.

He still felt bad remembering it now. But the truth was, he'd driven away from her apartment feeling free, and like he'd freed her, too, whether or not she realized it yet. And he hadn't thought about it all that much in the two days since.

Instead he'd focused on building this stage and...trying not to think too much about a certain country songbird who would soon be performing there. Pretty hard, though, given the logistics. That he was building this *for her.* So of course she was on his mind. *I never got over you.* Damn, why couldn't he quit hearing that? But there it was, playing in his head like a broken country record.

On the third day, no note.

But also no '58 Chevy. So she was at work but had quit leaving notes.

Which was probably good. For many reasons. And he refused to admit to himself that maybe he missed finding one just a little.

Heading back down the hill, he got to work—adding two

angled back walls that left space in between for a view of the grounds behind and a little air flow for those searing South Carolina days and nights.

And speaking of searing—by noon the sun blazed. A sign that spring had arrived in Low Country for sure—making each day a little hotter. When sweat started rolling down his chest, he laid his hammer on the brand new stage floor and yanked off the t-shirt he wore, then rolled it up and tied it around his head to keep the sweat from his eyes. Tomorrow, cargo shorts, but for today he was stuck in blue jeans.

Back to work. Given that there was no one to worry about bothering, he turned on some music, letting it blare from his phone to make the time go faster. He chose some old school eighties rock from around the time he was born, like Rick often played in his bar—starting with a little Def Leppard.

Drawing a few nails from the pouch at his side, he let the music guide the rhythm of his hammer. It made the work go quicker, even as the temps rose higher and the perspiration rolled down his back.

Josie wasn't trying to sneak up on him, but she could tell he hadn't noticed her arrival as she'd approached. And now she stood behind him saying his name. But he couldn't hear over the music.

After three tries, she gave up—and just watched. It was a nice view. Too nice. She'd seen him naked the other day, but that had been fleeting and so full of every kind of sensation that she hadn't gotten to simply enjoy looking.

Now she took in the muscles in his arms, shiny with sweat. She took in broad shoulders and a strong back—and even covered in blue jeans, she remembered what a nice ass he had. She bit her lip, unable to stop staring. She'd come out just to be nice—with a bottle of water, because it was hot and maybe he didn't have any. He'd had a shirt on when she'd made that decision. And then—boom—she'd come out the door and he hadn't been wearing it anymore.

Everything inside her pulsated. Maybe she should have stayed in the house. Hell, maybe she should have stayed in Nashville—and perhaps she would have if she'd had any idea he would still affect her this way. Yes, she'd never gotten over him, but apparently she'd forgotten the raw magnetism between them. And she thought perhaps it had even increased with age, or time apart, or something. But the reason didn't matter—what mattered, in that moment, was the fierce need running like wildfire through her body.

Take a deep breath, get hold of yourself. You came out here to give him water—so give him water. She took a step forward and, waiting until his hammer wasn't in a raised position, gently tapped him on the shoulder.

He swung around with a start, then his eyes locked on hers. Only for a second, though, before they ran the length of her. Then came back to her face as he reached to silence the music on his phone, leaving the air still and instantly thick with tension. "I thought you were gone," he said.

"I was. Running errands. Now I'm back."

"This is what you wear to run errands?"

She glanced down at herself. Short, raveled cut-offs, and an old sleeveless blouse tied at the waist. "No," she told him, "this is what I wear to mow the lawn. Which is what I'm about to do. But it's hot out, so I thought first I'd…" She held out the bottle of water by way of explanation.

"Oh. Thanks, but I…" He motioned over his shoulder to a cooler she hadn't noticed, sitting near a toolbox on the stage floor.

"Oh." She lowered the bottle. And said, "The stage is, uh, looking amazing. I, um…" *Am dreadfully distracted by how much I want you right now.* "I can't wait to, uh…"

"Aw, damn it, Josie," he muttered. Then let his hammer drop to the ground as he reached for her.

CHAPTER SEVEN

*S*he couldn't have pushed him away if she'd wanted to. And God knew she didn't want to. As his mouth came down on hers, hard, demanding, she melted into him beneath the hot sun—complete surrender to any and everything he wanted from her. *This is happening again, really happening again. I get to have him again. One more time.* It was like suffering from starvation and suddenly having a grand buffet set before you.

But only this once—so as they kissed and touched and grinded and groaned, She tried to drink in every sensation, every detail. The stubble on his chin beneath her fingertips. The smell of perspiration on his skin. The taste of his mouth. The heaving of her chest as he ripped open her shirt, buttons flying. The heaving of his as she kissed her way down it, all the way to his zipper. The low, hot moan that left him as she took his hard length into her hand. And then between her lips. The sound of him whispering her name up above.

Soon she whispered his name, too, as he laid her back on the stage, parted her legs, and kissed her where she wet for him. *I love you. I love you. I love you.* Each time she whispered, "Tanner," that was what she really meant.

She shut her eyes and sank utterly into the moment, the pleasure, as he made her come with his mouth—and then he was turning her over, using his hands to position her, facing her away from him on the stage, on her knees. He stood in the grass just below the elevated platform, hands splayed on her bare hips as he buried himself inside her, filling her with that oh-so-wonderfully solid part of him. Nothing had ever felt better or more right in her life than having Tanner inside her. Ever. Even going to Nashville. *I should have stayed. I should have stayed. I never should have given you up.*

The joining of their bodies was, for her, profound. They moved beneath the scorching sun in the most primal of rhythms, Josie crying out at each powerful thrust he delivered, welcoming it with her body, and with her heart. Somehow it felt even more perfect to connect with him this way here, at Rosebud, the place where they'd spent so much time falling in love, than if it had happened anyplace else.

She didn't know how long they moved that way together, her body absorbing the deep plunges that reverberated all through her, out to the tips of her fingers and toes—she only knew the consuming pleasure that came with them.

When he withdrew, she let out a whimper at the loss, needing him back inside her so, so bad—but then she realized he was only turning her over again, now lying her back on the stage in the blazing sunshine.

She barely felt the hard planks beneath her when he re-entered her waiting body—there was nothing but the bliss of having him back where she needed him, driving deep, deep, deep into her welcoming flesh.

When finally he came, his body collapsing gently atop her with a spent groan, she'd never felt more fulfilled. This was where she belonged. Not just at Rosebud. But with Tanner.

He might refuse to let that happen, and she still couldn't blame him, but nothing would ever be this right.

He pulled out and rolled onto his back next to her, same as before.

"So…no condom," she gently ventured. There hadn't been the last time, either.

"Things were a little rushed," he said. Then he turned his head to peer over at her. "And I thought you didn't like them anyway." In their youth, they'd used them faithfully—until she'd started on birth control pills and she'd liked it so much better without.

"I still don't, but sometimes it's…a necessity."

"I've always been careful, safe, with other people," he assured her.

Though it should register relief, instead the words made something inside her cringe—at the very thought of him doing this with anyone else. But she shoved it down. It had been seven years—they'd both had other lovers. She only knew that, for her, no one had ever made her feel the way he did. "Me, too, so…I guess it's fine that we're not using them."

"This can't happen again, Josie."

It felt like a punch to the gut. She blew a sigh up into the warm afternoon air. She'd known good and well he felt that way—she'd even reminded herself when it had started that it would surely be only this one more indulgence—yet she found herself throwing his words in his face. "That's what you said last time."

"And I meant it. And I mean it even more now."

"Because of the girlfriend who isn't a girlfriend?" she ventured, albeit a bit more gingerly than the last time she'd asked.

"No," he said, "I broke up with her."

Hallelujah! That was sweet music to Josie's ears.

Then he sat upright on the bare wood of the stage floor,

and ran a hand back through his thick hair. "I just can't seem to be around you without…"

The confession filled her with a fresh, feminine sort of joy, even when he trailed off. He might not like what he was saying, but *she* did. Because if he couldn't be around her without this happening, then it *would* happen again. And again. And again. Until he finally quit fighting it. Still, she played lip service to what he claimed to want. "Then I guess it's good I wasn't here the last couple of days." She sat up as well, pulling her blouse together and reaching for her shorts.

"Yeah, kept things a little simpler, that's for sure." His pants had never actually come off this time, so now he got to his feet to zip them. "And by the way…" He glanced up toward the road. "Josie, you can't just leave notes on your front gate telling any passerby the place is unlocked."

"There *aren't* any passersby," she smartly pointed out.

He took a second, clearly realizing she was right, but then held up one finger. "The mailman."

She tipped her head back. "Well, if the mailman wants to steal some Pop Tarts, old dishes, and a sagging La-Z-Boy—which are some of the exciting highlights of the house's contents—then it's his lucky day. But I don't even have mail service yet—just officially changed my address at the post office today, in fact. So we're clear of the thieving mailman."

At this, he sat back down on the edge of the stage near her and looked around. "Why do you have to live somewhere so damn secluded?"

She tilted her head, confused. "Huh?"

"If you lived about anywhere else," he explained, "we wouldn't be able to do this without worrying someone would see."

She shrugged. "One of Rosebud's many charms."

"I used to think so," he confessed.

And she decided to change the subject away from him

thinking sex with her was such a bad thing. "I'm really happy to be here at home again. It's going to take me a while to fix the house up the way I want inside, but I have plans to paint some walls, put up some new curtains, maybe buy a piano and make a music room."

He turned to cast her a skeptical look. "You don't play the piano."

"I do *now*, a little. I took lessons in Nashville."

His expression went dry and judgmental. "Where you were too broke to live."

She shrugged once more, and neither one of them had to say it: typical Josie. Then she made a hopeful suggestion. "Maybe I can play for you sometime."

"Maybe." But it sounded more like no.

She wasn't deterred, though. It was that love elation driving her forward. "Can...can I go get my guitar and play some songs for you? I miss sharing my music with you, Tanner."

"You're the one who left and quit sharing it."

Ouch. But still, completely deserved. She just hadn't seen it coming. Love elation could blind you. "My biggest mistake," she told him.

And he relented with, "Fine—go get it."

She smiled. "Thank you." Then scurried up the hill barefoot, not even bothering to hunt down the old tennis shoes she'd kicked off in the heat of passion. Two minutes later she came skittering back through the soft grass, old guitar case in hand.

Setting it on the stage floor, she undid the buckles, flipped open the lid, and lifted her guitar from the deep blue velvet interior—the once plush fabric long since flattened by time, but she'd always liked the blue since it was a little different than most cases.

"You still have that same old beat-up guitar from the

pawn shop?" She glanced up to see surprise flicker across Tanner's handsome face.

Though she didn't really understand it. "What else would I be playing?" He'd driven her to the pawn shop with fifty dollars she'd gotten for her birthday when they were both seventeen.

"Um, something newer and better?" he suggested.

She looked down at the instrument, the wood worn and scratched, faded to an entirely different color than the rest in some spots, the finish long gone. She never even noticed those things about it, though, until a moment like this when someone pointed them out. "No, I love this guitar," she said with complete conviction. You helped me pick it out. I'll always play it."

The memory of buying the guitar together brought to mind an old song she'd written for him, all the way back then, when they were in high school and had just fallen in love. She strummed the first notes of the simple ballad and began to sing.

"There's only you...when I feel lonely,
There's only you...when I'm let down,
There's only you...when I need holding,
You're the only one I'll always want around."

She felt his eyes on her hands as she plucked at the guitar strings, the melody to this song more intricate than most she'd written.

It felt magical to play for him again. He'd always been happy to listen, to encourage her, and they'd spent many a summer afternoon sitting in the grass this way, many a night beneath the stars as well, her playing for him in the moonlight. The fact that she knew he truly loved her music had been one more way they'd connected on a soul-deep level.

But maybe she'd picked the wrong song. Because even as she sang, the recollections and emotions it brought up spilled out through her voice. Her chest went tight. She should have sung something lighter, like the pink roses song she was working on. But she'd chosen one, carelessly, that harkened back to a time when they were young and in love and thought they had a lifetime of happiness before them.

When she finished, she stilled her hand, flattening it across the guitar strings, and kept her eyes down. To let the emotion pass.

That was when his deep voice cut through the fresh silence. "I'm sorry, Josie. But I can't."

She looked up, met his gaze. "Can't what?"

"This is...too much like old times. I gotta go."

And like that, he was off, leaving behind his tools, his cooler...and her.

$\sim$

THE YARD DIDN'T GET MOWED that day. Josie had too much on her mind. And songs to write. The curse of a songwriter was that they were everywhere—in everything. It had been the reason she couldn't turn in homework in high school and it was why she couldn't stay on task now, either. Before the day was done she'd written two, a ballad called "The Last to Leave," and a more bluesy tune entitled "If This Guitar Could Talk," about each scratch and scar being a memory.

The blessing of the songs was that they served as a distraction, and they often helped her work through her emotions—or at least allowed her to channel them into something that felt productive.

So it wasn't until darkness fell and she was reheating left-over pizza for dinner that she really stopped and let herself *feel* everything that had happened. And as she slumped into an old kitchen chair at an old table that had been left behind, part of her felt devastated. That Tanner refused to even consider forgiving her, even consider giving them a chance to be together again. And he had her on an emotional roller-coaster—up, down, up, down—everything seemed to change by the moment with him since she'd come home.

And the worst part was—she still knew she deserved it. She'd done something awful to him. And the way she'd done it had allowed her to spend all those years in Nashville never having to face the fallout. And this—now—was the fallout. So she had no right to complain, no leg to stand on in the this-isn't-fair department.

Though…if great sex could be considered fallout—well, many women wouldn't consider that so bad. And God knew she wouldn't trade these last two hot, glorious encounters with him for anything. Both her body and her heart had been sated, and she never could have imagined something like this happening when she'd rolled back up the lane to Rosebud, eking the last half mile out of that empty gas tank. And even if this was all she ever had of him…well, it was more than she'd had a week ago. And she supposed she could look on it as a bit of closure—hot, steamy, urgent closure—that neither of them had gotten up to now.

If only her heart could quit aching for more. For the way they once were. For the love that had gone bone deep for them both—no questions, no worries, just utter devotion. Once upon a time, they'd been the couple everyone wanted to be. And then she'd ruined it. And maybe she'd *never* get over that. She hadn't so far anyway.

Though even while she knew to her core that she'd hurt him so, so badly, she couldn't help but wonder: When did *she* earn the right to feel hurt in return? And what about uncon-ditional love? If he'd loved her so very much back then, shouldn't he be able to forgive her *now*? But maybe there were things *he'd* never get over, either.

Fortunately, however, by the time she finished her pizza,

another part of her—the part of her that always held on to hope—started feeling just a little bit happy again. Remembering that he'd come back. Because he couldn't *not* come back.

And *one* round of urgent sex—that was a way to seek closure, a way to say a final goodbye and move on. But twice was…a pattern.

And as she lay her plate in the sink and crushed a soda can before dropping it in the trash, her soul sung with all the hot electricity that drew them together. It was the most amazing feeling on the planet—what else could leave you feeling tingly and happy and warm all just while standing at the kitchen sink—and she knew he felt it, too.

Even if she hated the way he left, the more she thought about the whole situation, the happier she slowly became. It was the return of that wonderful giddiness—that love elation. *It's okay because he'll be back. And I don't have to work tomorrow. And he can't resist me. And sooner or later he'll give in to that—he'll see it's okay to trust in that. We'll go slow and I'll prove myself to him.*

Well, okay, maybe we can't really go slow—we've already had urgent sex twice—but I'll figure out how to make him see that I would never leave him again.

She fell asleep happy, new tunes rippling through her mind even as anticipation rippled across her skin. Suddenly, she wasn't even sure why she'd been sad before—once she got a little perspective on the situation, she realized it was all going perfectly for her. Despite that she'd hurt him horribly, already he'd forgiven her enough to build an amphitheater for her, he'd had sex with her twice, and they'd even started talking through things and catching up on what they'd missed in each other's lives.

The next morning, she again chose clothes conducive to mowing the yard. She really had to take care of it today—her family had hired someone to do it while no one was living here, but she'd insisted that she take care of it going forward. This was her place now and she was going to take responsibility for the upkeep. The grounds were expansive, but a big riding mower still sat in the tool shed, along with a push mower for trim work.

She put on the same raveled denim shorts from yesterday, and a thin pink tank top over a hot pink bra, all the while singing a song she'd written long ago—at another time when Tanner had been full of doubt and caution but she'd refused to let it bring her down, instead using it for inspiration.

"There's a thousand broken hearts in this city,

A thousand broken hearts who never tried,

There's a thousand broken hearts crying for what they could have been,

A thousand broken hearts and one of 'em's mine."

She put her hair in a ponytail, still singing, then came downstairs. She'd just grabbed a bottle of water from the fridge and was just about to merrily embark on her task—when a knock came on the front door.

As she approached, she spotted Tanner through the glass on the top half of the door and the sheer curtain that covered it. Her heart bloomed with fresh affection for him—even if it surprised her to see him there; she'd assumed he'd just start back to work and make a half-hearted effort to avoid her. But if he wasn't avoiding, all the better.

She whisked open the old cottage green wooden door with a smile. "Hey," she greeted him.

"Hey." He didn't smile. But that didn't daunt her. She was getting used to his seesawing behavior. He'd be back grinning in his old, friendly Tanner way soon enough.

"What's up? Need the bathroom? Or anything else?" She continued smiling. Trying not to be flirty—lest it look like she was attempting to manipulate or seduce him—but also making it clear she'd put his hasty departure yesterday behind them and was cheerfully moving on.

"No—I wanted to introduce you to Steve," he said—and a glance to his right brought another guy stepping up into view.

"Oh." She tried not to appear taken back. "Hi, Steve."

"Nice to meet you, miss." The other man was a little older —forty-something, with graying hair and a slight paunch, and struck her as shy but polite.

"Steve's one of my foremen," Tanner told her. "His crew just finished up a room addition, so they're going to help out here—get the benches in, and the rest of the stage up."

"Oh, okay—great." Maybe not really *great*—but fine. She'd known he couldn't do the entire job on his own anyway— he'd old her that. So he'd have some help now. And sure, this meant there probably wouldn't be anymore impulsive, outdoor sex in the immediate future, but he'd still be here working, and they'd still see each other, and that was the important thing. And who knew—maybe there *would* be times he'd end up here alone, early, or late. So this wasn't ideal—but it was okay.

"Steve will be overseeing the rest of the project while I tend to other things," Tanner said then. "Should be done in a few weeks."

"Oh." So he *wouldn't* be here. Which meant so much more than a boss "tending to other things." This was him saying: *What I told you yesterday is for real. I can resist you. And this is how I'm doing it.*

She feared her devastation was written all over her face even as she said, "Wow, that's speedy."

"It's a pretty simple project, all things considered," he pointed out, "and now that we have a whole crew on it, it'll go fast."

"Well, that's…great," she said again.

"Steve's been with me for the better part of ten years," Tanner went on. "Knows what he's doing, so you can trust him to get the job done right—and if you have any questions, he'll be onsite here every day 'til it wraps up."

As if she gave a crap about any of that. "Great, great," she murmured as she nodded. Great: code word for I-can't-summon-any-other-words-at-the-moment.

"So I'll just grab my tools and cooler," he said, pointing absently in the general direction of where he'd left them yesterday, "and take off—and Steve and his guys will get to work."

One more nod. "Great."

~

THE LAST THING she wanted to do today now was mow the damn yard. But the spring grass was getting taller every day, and she was officially a homeowner now, and she had to prove—to herself and to her family—that she could handle it.

She filled the mower's tank with gas from the can she'd toted to a station a few days ago. *No more empty gas tanks around here, no way—I'm practical Josie now.* Even if Tanner's departure had left her crushed. *Funny, I left him one time seven years ago, and now he keeps leaving me over and over again.* She glanced to the sky, pretty sure there was a song in that thought.

But as she commenced mowing, another one quickly filled her head, and she sang it out loud as she worked, despite the crew of six men toiling on her property—no one would hear her over the sound of the mower.

"Well, I'm mowin' and I'm cryin' and I'm thinkin' and I'm wishin' that I never would've run away from you.

And I'm wishin' and I'm thinkin' as I'm cryin' that I'm knowin' that my broken heart will forever now be blue."

She was pretty sure she couldn't seriously make a song about mowing grass, but the tune kept her working, kept her driving the mower all over the big yard trying to pretend everything was normal. Because, after all, if they hadn't had sex—if he'd simply done this construction job for her, giving her this idea and a chance for a new start at what she loved— this *would* be normal. She'd be happy, excited about the stage and the benches and all the music the clearing might soon hold. And she'd be thinking that this was just one more big change—toward a wonderful new life.

But we did have sex.

And sex bonded you with someone, like it or not.

And what made it even more complicated was that, despite herself, she did like it—because she loved him and *wanted* to be bonded. She'd never really *stopped* being bonded with him. And the sex had just…cemented it. Made that bond new and fresh and alive and real.

Until he'd walked away for good this morning.

She'd felt that—the finality. He was serious this time.

He wouldn't come back tomorrow. Or the day after that. He'd keep his distance and try to let that bond wear thin. And who knew—maybe he'd even get back together with the girl- friend who wasn't a girlfriend. Because she was safer. *She'd* never gotten in a truck and driven away from him without a word.

She was probably better for him. *Because you, Josie Bell, are a wreck. You're a big unpredictable, undependable, flighty, irre- sponsible, impractical, selfish, whim-following wreck of a person who doesn't deserve a steady, true, loving guy like Tanner Rose.*

And the weird thing was—she'd spent the last seven years knowing that, and being okay with it. Accepting herself for who she was. Someone who had chosen her music over her man. But somehow now it was harder, hurt even more. Because she was trying to be better. Wanted with her whole heart to be better. And knew that she could, would, succeed at that. So the part that hurt was understanding for sure now that it was really too late with Tanner, and that no matter what she did or who she became, they'd never be together again.

That night she tried to write down some of the songs in her head—but a strange thing happened. The distraction the music usually brought her...didn't come. Instead, she started crying and couldn't stop. Maybe because she was crying for seven years of loss and heartbreak and mistakes. She couldn't go back and fix anything, make anything right. She cried until she gave up on stopping, on writing down the music, and lay down in bed, the guitar still in her grasp. She woke up with her arms wrapped around it.

She loved that guitar, but it was a hell of a lot colder and harder to hold onto than Tanner. *And this is what I traded him for. This is what I'm left with. This is all I have now—the music.* Once upon a time, she'd thought that was enough. But now she knew she was wrong.

CHAPTER EIGHT

*O*ver the next few weeks, the amphitheater came together beautifully. Josie got in the habit of walking down to the construction site most nights after the crew departed and taking in how the grounds of Rosebud were changing.

The half-log benches were installed, along with electricity that ran from the gatehouse, and some lighting. The stage awning was added, covered with old-fashioned gray slate roofing tiles, along with a warm stain on the entirety of the wood structure that made it feel older and a little weathered —in a good way. She sat on the stage, sometimes remembering how she and Tanner had christened it and knowing that would always be their secret—and other times playing her guitar and singing, trying the space on for size. At still other times, she rested on the benches, peering down at the stage, imagining what it would be like to sit in the audience, albeit hearing the music only in her head.

She wrote a lot during the period. The songs were no substitution for Tanner, for love, but her music really did feel like all she had left. She continued working at the grocery, saving what little bits of money she could after living expenses, and she spent her days off getting the house more in order. She bought some second hand furniture for the living room and graciously accepted a TV from Daphne that her sister swore came from a guestroom no one ever used.

She took three old jars from the kitchen cabinets and labeled them *Tanner*, *Daphne*, and *Mom and Dad*. And she dropped a few dollars or coins in each every few days, whatever she could spare. She knew there were many more modern, technological ways of paying people back and better places to keep your money, but something about this system made her feel more accountable. Keeping her debts right in front of her on the kitchen windowsill would help her pay them off, bit by bit. She decided once a month she'd empty the jars, deposit the money in the bank, and write checks out to her "lenders." Whether that check was for fifty dollars or ten, it would make a dent and show everyone she intended to make good.

She tracked down the other musical acts Tanner had told her about and started on plans for a grand opening of the amphitheater that would feature a triple bill: herself, the Backroad Boys bluegrass band, and Denver Ellis.

As luck would have it, the Backroad Boys' mandolin player possessed an art background and agreed to make a quaint sign for the new gate that led to the amphitheater—as soon as she settled on a name. He understood her financial situation and promised not to bill her until after the show.

She made flyers on her laptop, posting them at the grocery, the library, and all over town—anyplace she could find to put one up. And she drove to surrounding towns and did the same. She asked Delia and anyone else she came into contact with to spread the word. She wasn't sure it would work, but she was depending partly on the other two acts having local followings, and partly on the idea that maybe people would be drawn out of curiosity to see Josie Bell, that crazy girl who went running off to Nashville and broke Tanner Rose's heart only to come home with nothing left to do but sing in her very own backyard—literally.

Of course, the real question had become—for her—who broke whose heart in the end? Because every move she made during those weeks waiting for the amphitheater to be completed was done with an anchor chained around her heart. Or that's what it felt like anyway—and as if she might be pulled under by the weight of it at any moment. She knew how to paste on a smile when she needed to—hard times in Music City had taught her to put on a show, appear happy when sad, strong when weak—but underneath it all her soul ached for all the happiness she could have had with Tanner.

She was pushing forward because she had to. There was no other choice. But this was a wound time wouldn't heal, music wouldn't heal, nothing would heal.

SHE'D RETURNED home from Delia's last night to find a note taped to her door. From Steve. Telling her the job was finished.

The grand opening show was two weeks away, so it was a relief to have it done. The last step was the pink roses. So the next day she drove to the Rose Family Nursery and Garden Center—the only place nearby that would have what she needed, so she couldn't really avoid it—and found herself saying hello to Tanner's brother, Jace. He was friendly, and she inquired about his recent honeymoon. And then he asked, "You here for the roses?"

She blinked. "How did you know?"

"Tanner asked me to order in twenty containers of climbing pink roses and twenty more bushes. For the climbers, I went with Zephirine Drouhins. A mouthful, I know. But they're thornless and'll grow six to twelve feet. I got Knock Outs for the bushes, because they're just easy—super low maintenance."

She blinked again, taken aback. "Tanner asked you to...?"

"To put around the stage," he explained, as if he knew the situation better than she did, leaving her to feel a little dumb.

"I just had no idea he'd done that." She shook her head.

"Oh. Is it okay? If you don't like those varieties, I can—"

"No—no, it's great," she said. And this time she really *meant* great. She was a little blown away by the gesture, in fact. But then she bit her lip. "Though I'm not sure I can afford that many right now—I had planned to start out a little smaller in scope."

To her further surprise, however, Jace simply waved away her concerns. "No worries—Tanner said to bill him and he'll add it to your invoice. And since he's family, you're getting them for wholesale prices." He ended with a cheerful wink.

Still rather dazed by the turn of events, she concluded her business with Jace—which really just amounted to helping him load all the roses into the bed of her pickup. It took two trips home and a lot of toting large containers around, but she wasn't complaining. The theater area was large, and having so many more roses to work with than she'd planned on was going to make it much prettier much quicker, and much more matching to the "rosebud" part of the name—even if she still hadn't decided on the *exact* name just yet.

As she drove out of Jace's lot with the second and last load of roses, the back of her truck literally filled to over-flowing with pink blooms, her heart brimmed with still more love for Tanner. He'd thought of everything, right down to the flowers. Just like on the night he'd proposed.

But stop, don't go there. You've got roses to plant—a crapload of them!—and a show to put on. Stay focused. For once in your life, stay practical and focused and make this all work.

~

THE NEXT DAY an April sun blazed down on Rosebud and its brand new theater. Josie knelt on the ground, freeing the first climbing rose from its plastic pot to lower it in the hole she'd just dug. Tanner's crew had added mulch, but she'd swept it aside with a rake and would push it back up around the plant's base when she was done.

Her back ached by the time she took a lunch break, but she kept the rest time short and got back to work, determined to plant them all today, since it was supposed to rain tomorrow. It would be nice for them to get a thorough soaking in their new soil. She wasn't sure she would make it —it was a lot of work—but she'd give it her best. She hummed "Pink Roses"—which she'd long since finished—as she worked, and soon was belting out the tune in earnest. Another perk of living someplace off the beaten path—she'd always felt at ease to sing as loudly as she pleased at Rosebud. And so it seemed fitting she'd soon be doing that here professionally. As long as someone showed up to listen, anyway.

It was she only as she paused between stanzas and turned to reach for her shovel that she saw Tanner walking toward her.

She went silent. Spoke quietly. "I didn't hear your truck." And her heart began beating so fast, just at the sight of him, that it nearly took her breath away.

"Singing pretty loud, I guess," he said.

"Sorry," she murmured.

"No, I like it. Nice song."

"It's about…um…"

"Pink roses," he finished for her.

She nodded dumbly. And decided maybe she'd do better at getting words out if she just spoke the ones on her mind at the moment. "I'm surprised to see you."

"I wanted to get a peek at the place, see how it turned out." He stopped a few feet in front of her, then took a long look around before lowering his gaze back to hers. "Do you like it?"

Something about his tone whisked her back to their youth. He seemed boyish, sweet, like he sought her approval for something he'd given her. He'd asked her the same question about the engagement ring he'd slid onto her finger on the front lawn. And the 1958 Chevy he'd so painstakingly restored for her.

She gave the same answer now that she'd given the other times. "I love it. It's perfect."

"Yeah, I think it's nice, too. I'm glad you like it."

"It's a beautiful addition to the property," she said, "and yet it fits so well here that it feels like it's been a part of the place forever. It's...well, more than I ever could have dreamt up or put together on my own. So thank you."

He gave a short nod in reply, nothing more.

"Now I only have to fill it with people," she said, adding a shaky sigh. It suddenly seemed like a tall order now that the amphitheater had become a reality.

"You'll fill it. You'll fill it to overflowing." Spoken with the same conviction of knowing the sun would rise tomorrow.

"You really think so?" she asked, doubt still threatening her confidence.

"I know so."

"How?"

He tilted his head, met her gaze. "I've never known anybody to be more passionate about anything. That's the kind of passion that moves mountains, Jos."

She drew in a deep breath, blew it back out, grateful for his faith. Then she remembered to ask him something that had been on her mind for weeks. "You never told me which name you like best. The Rosebud Theater, the Rosebud Stage, or the Stage at Rosebud."

Clearly he'd been thinking about it—since he didn't hesitate. "The Rosebud Stage. More original than the first option. Less of a mouthful than the last."

She smiled. "Thank you. The Rosebud Stage it is."

It pleased her, and would always please her, for him to have chosen the name.

"Need some help with the rest of these roses?" he offered. About ten pots remained. "I'll dig, you plant?"

"I'll take you up on that," she said. Not only because it was nice having him there, but for practical reasons. Finally, she was learning to think practically. "I'm trying to beat the rain."

"No funny business, though," he said, pointing at her with the index finger of one hand while he took the shovel from her with the other.

She gave her best aloof shrug. "First of all, I never *started* the funny business. And second, I would never describe the business of which you speak as funny. But agreed. I'm all about getting these roses in the ground before dark."

She'd started the project by placing the roses where she wanted them to go, so he didn't have to ask where to dig. And as he got started, he said, "Sing me some songs while we work, Josie."

So she sang. Staying away from sad ones this time, and sticking to her more upbeat tunes or covers of songs on the radio. They worked companionably, but it was probably wise that he labored at a distance from her, sometimes separated by twenty or thirty yards across the wide space the amphitheater stretched.

Soon climbing roses were planted all along the stage's

angled sides, the gatehouse that was becoming an office and ticket window, and the newly erected signpost that only awaited a sign now that she officially had a name. The bushes lined the picket fence near the brand new gate and dotted open areas.

Of course, he finished the holes before she caught up with him, so he began planting a few of the remaining roses himself, starting at the opposite end of the area where she worked—until they met in the middle of the row along the fence. He lowered the last bush in its hole, and together they knelt next to it to push the loose soil back in with their hands, patting it down.

Their hands brushed, touched each other as they packed the last rose bush into its new spot—and good Lord, how those touches skittered all through her. She'd been working in the hot sun all day, she was sweaty and gross, and her shoulders, back, and thighs were killing her—so she truly wouldn't have believed anything could arouse her right now. But when they both lifted their gazes—and it turned out their faces were only inches apart, and she could smell everything musky and masculine about him, she discovered that even now, like this, he possessed the ability to turn her on.

Make her want.

Make her breath go shallow.

Make the spot between her thighs ache.

His blue eyes smoldered on her, appearing more the color of midnight in the shadows beneath the late afternoon sun. He'd said no funny business, but now she could only conclude that he hadn't meant it. That he'd come back for a different reason than he'd claimed. Like before, he'd been unable to resist, the magnetism between them too powerful for him to push down.

She bit her lip, their gazes still locked, as the desire spiraled through her. Her chest constricted. *This is happening again. This amazing connection with the love of my life is happening again.*

That was when he pulled his hand back, pushed abruptly to his feet, took a couple steps back.

So she forced herself to stand quickly up, too.

"All done," he said.

With everything. That was what his commanding tone added on. No funny business for real. He hadn't come back for that, after all.

And maybe it should have made her feel better that what had almost happened proved he really couldn't be around her without wanting her again. But the fact that he was resisting this time negated that.

And still, no matter what emotions twisted and tangled and tightened inside her right now, she had no choice but to respect his decision—and to remember the big picture here. The big picture of what he'd done for her over the past month since she'd come home. So she took a deep breath, steeled herself, and said, "Thank you. For the help. For all of this. For everything. I'll forever be grateful, Tanner."

"You're welcome, Josie," he told her. And with that, turned to walk away.

And maybe she should just let him go. He'd proven, after all, that it was what he really wanted. But she wasn't sure when—or if—she'd see him again, and something rose up inside her, compelling her to take one last shot at happiness with him. "There's something else I'm just as passionate about, Tanner," she boldly announced behind him.

He stopped, looked over his shoulder at her.

And she went for broke. "I never stopped loving you and I want you back. I was wrong to go the way I did—so, so wrong—but my love for you never faded. And I know you feel it, too."

"No," he said simply.

All the air left her lungs, making it hard to breathe. "No, you don't feel it?"

He shook his head. "No, I can't be in a relationship with you again."

"But Tanner, I—"

He cut her off. "How could I ever trust you again, Josie? How? I can't, that simple." He stopped, dropped his glance to the ground, gave his head another shake, and then lifted his eyes back to her. He looked sad. "And...I just can't be around you anymore, Jos. I'm sorry, but I can't, so this has to be goodbye. Knock 'em dead on the Rosebud Stage—I know you will and I wish you the best."

She watched numbly as he turned to go, and she didn't try to stop him this time. She'd put it out there, put it on the line —and so had he. It was really over for good. And the worst part was the same as always—she knew it was all her fault.

CHAPTER NINE

*T*anner sat at a table with his entire family, sulking. Trying not to, since they were celebrating his parents' fortieth wedding anniversary at Salty Pete's, but it wasn't working. Maybe because it was just difficult right now to be surrounded by all this devoted, committed, romantic happiness. It was a little easier to shove it all aside when he was working—hammering nails, sawing wood—it took just enough focus to drive away thoughts of what was missing. But here, with his newlywed brother and wife, and his soon-to-be-married brother and bride—not to mention the two lovebirds who'd given birth to them—he was starting to feel like the odd man out.

"A toast to the Rose family," Rick said, lifting a frosty mug of beer.

"Hear hear," their father said, and they all clinked glasses and mugs and took hearty drinks.

Conversation was lively and brisk across the long table in the open-air restaurant—Shelby announced that she'd taken a job at a small ad agency on nearby Johns Island, and Mia was bubbling with wedding talk—she and Rick would take their vows late next month at the Sassafras Presbyterian Church, a quaint old structure just off Main Street.

His brothers had found women who were, well...easy to love. No rocky stops and starts, no breakups to make up, no big emotional rollercoaster—once they were together and committed, they'd stayed that way, there for each other, always. Tanner wanted *that* kind of woman, that kind of life. Even as much as he hated feeling a little envious of his older brothers, he couldn't deny it. He wanted what he'd once *thought* he had with Josie.

After the meal, the ladies made for the bathroom, and Rick and Dad had their heads together talking about a mechanical problem on Rick's pickup. Jace slid into an empty seat next to Tanner. "You're weird tonight, bro. Quiet. It's creeping me out a little."

True that Tanner wasn't usually the sullen type.

"Trouble in Josieville?"

Tanner had filled Jace in on the situation when he'd placed the order for the roses. "I *left* Josieville, remember? Never to return."

"Yeah, and I'm guessing that's what has you in a funk."

He shrugged. "More or less. Guess I just wish she was more like Shelby or Mia."

At this, Jace's eyebrows shot up. "You say that like those two are quiet little waifs. Trust me—Shelby is nobody's doormat. And I wouldn't want her that way."

But Tanner shook his head. "Oh, I know that. What I meant was—once you were together, you stayed that way. I know there was some drama getting to that point, but once you were a couple, you were devoted, unwavering, all that— what a partner is supposed to be. And with Josie...well, there's no having that, ever. And that's why I can't go there." He met his brother's gaze. "Truth is, I almost wish she'd stayed in Nashville, hit it big and all that. If she'd never come back, I wouldn't have been reminded what I was missing."

Jace took all that in, seemed to think it over. "Only every time you turned on the radio," he pointed out.

"Fair enough." Hell if he knew *how* to get away from Josie. In ways, seemed like she was everywhere. Always had been.

"If it's devotion you're after," Jace said, "you could call up Ashlynn. I'm sure she'd take you back."

And Tanner shot him a sideways glance. He'd also told Jace how relieved he'd felt after breaking things off with her.

Jace simply shrugged. "Just sayin'."

Just saying maybe some things were more important than devotion? But without that, what did you really have? Passion, sure. Love—yeah, he still loved Josie, no doubt about that. And though he hadn't spent a ton of time with her since she'd come home, he was pretty sure they were still highly compatible. But without that last big piece of the pie, it didn't all hold together.

"Thing is, I'd never know for sure what tomorrow holds, and I'd always be waiting for the other shoe to drop. And who wants to live like that?"

"I get it," Jace said. "I really do. But..." He pushed back his chair, stood up. The group was reconvening, now ready to head to the Rose Tavern for cake and drinks. "The truth is...*none* of us really knows what tomorrow holds. We just think we do and have to have faith."

JOSIE COULD BARELY BELIEVE the time had come. The Rosebud Stage's inaugural show. Or at least she *hoped* it would be inaugural and that there'd be more to follow. Daphne and Mitch had kindly offered to work the ticket window so she could prepare to perform, and now she peeked out from the private area below the back of the stage to see...a packed house. She gasped. Then turned to Denver Ellis and the bluegrass band. "The place is full," she said, still stunned.

But none of them look surprised.

"I always said," Wally Devlin replied, "that if there was a place to play music around here, people would come. And here they are."

Josie bit her lip in cautious joy. *If you build it, they will come.* "This is amazing. Because I just wasn't sure. But I think the whole town is here. And maybe more. I...only hope they'll *keep* coming."

Wally gave her a grin, stroking his short beard. "We put on a good show tonight and they'll be back. Every damn weekend if you want it that way. I guarantee it."

Josie's heart filled with a new sort of happiness—a happiness that bordered on fulfillment. Tanner had been right—his idea, his vision, was on the verge of changing her life in a big way, for the better, maybe for a very long time to come. "Then let's put on a good show. Let's put on a *great* show!"

And with that, she pointed toward Carl, the sign painter and mandolin player, who was also serving as a makeshift announcer tonight. He spoke into the microphone in his hand, his voice echoing over the speakers Tanner's crew had installed. "Ladies and gentleman, please welcome to the stage Sassafras's own Miss Josie Bell."

And as Josie emerged onto her very own stage for the very first time, applause filled her ears. She went a little numb upon seeing all the people clapping, whistling, truly indeed welcoming her to the stage. And welcoming her home. She almost froze up—she'd never been in front of a crowd this large before. But she was a performer to the bone, so she quickly rolled with it, nerves be damned.

"Welcome, everybody, to the very first show on the Rosebud Stage."

More applause. Applause that made the skin on her arms tingle.

"I can't tell you all how very happy I am to be here with you, and I thank you from the bottom of my heart for coming out tonight." The words left her so smoothly that it was as if she'd been born to do this. "We have a great show planned for you on this beautiful spring evening…"

As she kept talking, she grew more comfortable on the stage and started taking in specific faces in the crowd. Her parents sat in the front row, Delia had brought a group, and true to her word, Susan McBeal had, too. She saw old friends and new, and many faces she'd never seen before tonight.

Against the better judgment of her heart, she'd been hoping maybe Tanner would come, just because it was the grand opening at the venue he'd created—or maybe even because he wanted to see how it went or hear her sing. But as she told the crowd a bit about the place, she realized he wasn't here. He hadn't come.

And she knew it shouldn't surprise her—but it left her a bit crestfallen anyway. Though she had no choice but to keep going, shove that to the back of her mind as much as possible, and do what she'd promised—put on a good show.

"We're gonna get things started with a brand new song I wrote just a few weeks ago—inspired by Rosebud itself, along with some memories—called, appropriately enough, 'Pink Roses.'"

∼

IT WAS WELL after dark when the anniversary celebration broke up and Tanner started driving home—until he found himself making a u-turn and heading in the opposite direction. Despite his best intentions, it was as if a magnet drew him—to the last place he wanted to be tonight.

The lane leading to Rosebud was packed with cars, far more than he'd even expected. Good—good for her. He was thankful he'd been right about this.

He wouldn't stay long, so he drove right past all the parked cars and up to the house, threw the truck in park, turned the key and got out. He wasn't even sure why he'd come. Just to see, he guessed. Just to see Josie in her glory, doing what she was born to do.

And as he quietly let himself in the gate and moved, unnoticed, in the shadows, to stand behind the last row beneath an old oak tree, it was a beautiful sight to behold. His Josie, looking like a star in a simple pair of blue jeans, a t-shirt, and a long fringed vest, sitting on a stool playing her guitar. She was finishing up a cover of an old song he knew she'd always loved: "Please, Mister, Please." She'd sung it when they were teenagers, driving along in his old Mustang, so old that it came without a radio or any other kind of music. *She* was the music. Then and now.

The crowd applauded when she finished, and as she spoke to them afterward, he was dumbstruck by how very clear it was that she belonged up on that stage. "That was a little Olivia Newton John, from back in 1974. I hadn't been born just yet, but when it comes to country music, they say I've got an old soul. I'd like to do one last song before we bring the Backroad Boys and Denver back out to do a few together. This is a brand new one I wrote just last week, about someone special I once loved—but lost."

Tanner's throat thickened with emotion when she started to sing.

I can't ask you to forgive,
I can't ask you to forget,
That I walked away from a love so true.
I know we're over now,
But I'll never know how,

To forgive myself for forgetting to love you."

Shit. He shouldn't have come. He felt too much for her, still. And hell—he probably always would.

He turned to go, the song she'd written for him still filling his ears—and his heart—all the way to the truck, until he got inside and slammed the door.

No more of this. No more Josie. No more Rosebud. No more.

CHAPTER TEN

$\mathcal{T}$anner sat at the bar in the Rose Tavern on a Friday night in May, nursing a beer, hanging out with his brothers a week before Rick's wedding, talking—at the moment—about some of the dirt tracks Jace would race on in the coming few months as the driver of the newly formed Rose Brothers Racing team. It was an easy, pleasant evening, the kind that took Tanner's mind off his troubles—the troubles that should have left him a long time ago given that he hadn't seen Josie since the opening night on the Rosebud Stage over a month back.

But damn, the girl stayed on his mind.

From what he'd heard, she'd continued to pack the place the last several weekends. And though he hadn't even billed her yet, she'd sent a check for a few hundred dollars to his company address, with a simple note that said:

A FIRST INSTALLMENT of many to start paying you back. Thank you again.

It surprised him not that she wanted to pay him back, but that she was so proactive about it. It impressed him simply that she was on top of the situation. Paying bills instead of writing songs.

The pleasant night, however, got shot to hell when Rick hung up from a phone call to say, "Shit—I can't believe this."

"What's wrong?" Jace asked, seated on a stool next to Tanner.

"Pipe burst at the church tonight." Rick let out a huge sigh. "It's flooded."

Jace's eyes went wide. "Whoa."

And Rick shook his head. "Mia's gonna be crushed."

"That's awful," Jace said.

Tanner didn't hold back from adding, "Looks like God has spoken." There had been a lot of joking around about Rick getting married in a church—he owned a bar and just wasn't the most traditionally religious guy around. But Mia had loved the character of the old building and wanted a classic wedding. Their mother had teased that she hoped God would let him in—and apparently the big guy had decided not to.

Rick glanced upward, and muttered dryly, "Really, God?" Then lowered his eyes back to his brothers. "What the hell am I gonna do about this without breaking Mia's heart? I mean, the woman's been patient with me—probably more often than I deserve. I wanted this to be perfect for her." He finished with another tired-looking shake of his head.

And Tanner heard himself asking, "How do you think she'd feel about an outdoor venue?"

Rick looked hopeful. "If it's nice, I'm sure she'd like it. I nixed that idea in the beginning, thinking of the heat and unpredictability of weather and all that."

Jace chimed in, looking at his phone, to say, "Well, no rain predicted next weekend, and looks like a high of seventy-five, part sun and part cloud. Can't get much better."

"You're right," Rick agreed, then looked back to Tanner. "What's the venue?"

"The Rosebud Stage." Which everyone in the family was well aware of by now. "Josie's been scheduling her shows on Friday nights—you could call her and see if it's free Saturday and what she would charge."

Rick narrowed his gaze on Tanner. "And it's as nice as you say?"

Tanner tilted his head. "Dude, I built the place. It's nice. Given your lack of options, you could do worse. I think Mia might actually love it."

"All right then," Rick said, wiping down the bar with a damp rag. "I better close up early and head home to break the news to her. And we'll call Josie in the morning." Then he stopped and looked back to Tanner. "You'd be okay with having to go there? For the wedding?"

It so happened that Rosebud was the last place Tanner wanted to go back to—ever. But it was a good solution to Rick's problem, so he didn't see that he had much of a choice. "I'll take one for the team," he said stiffly.

Josie couldn't believe Tanner's brother was getting married on her stage, but when he'd called about it, she'd said yes. Because Tanner himself had suggested that the venue might earn money other ways. And God knew she needed that money. And she felt terrible that the church had flooded —it was every woman's nightmare to have something ruin her wedding.

"How much?" Rick had asked her in his pointed way.

"Um, I'm not sure," she'd stammered. "I hadn't thought

about using it for a wedding." And she had no idea what the going rate for that sort of thing was.

"How about five hundred dollars?" he'd suggested.

She'd been about to say two hundred, but instead replied, "Yes—sure."

Later, she'd thought she should have just offered it up to him for free, all things considered, but now resolved that she'd just pay the five hundred straight back to Tanner as part of next month's installment.

Now the wedding day had arrived, so she threw on a decent dress—one of only a few she owned, it was springy and yellow. She wasn't invited or anything, so she planned to keep a low profile—but when Rick and Mia had come by on Monday to look at the place, Mia had asked if she could be on hand to help the musicians set up and that sort of thing.

When she saw a small gathering on the stage a couple of hours before the two-o'clock nuptials, she walked down, expecting to find the aforementioned musicians there—only to instead discover all three Rose brothers huddled with their parents and others involved in the ceremony. And no one looked happy. So much so that when she realized it, she stopped, hung back.

"I know what to do," she heard Tanner say to them all.

"What?" Rick asked. "Because I'm fresh out of water to keep putting out fires here." Clearly the venue change had taken a toll, and sounded like some other big new problem loomed on the horizon now.

Tanner answered by saying, "Josie."

Upon hearing her name, she blinked, stood up straighter. "Huh?"

At this, the group all glanced up toward her in unison—but mainly she saw Tanner. His face. His eyes. Handsome as ever, especially in a classic black tux. At his lapel he wore a single pink rosebud. "Singer lost her voice," Rick said, "and the harpist broke her leg just this morning."

"Wow," Josie murmured as Rick ran a hand forlornly back through his hair.

"Can you be the music?" Tanner asked her.

"Um—sure," she said. "I'll just need to know what to play —and when."

The woman she thought to be Jace's new wife stepped forward, holding out a sheet of paper. "This is a song list Mia gave the musicians."

Then Rick added, "But if you don't know them all, whatever you can play that makes sense for a wedding is fine. Seriously. I know this is last minute."

She took the song list and nodded. "Okay, I'll see what I can do."

"The only really important one," Rick said, "is that she wants to walk down the aisle to an instrumental version of 'I Can't Help Falling in Love With You.'"

Josie gave another nod. "Got it." Then she looked around, suddenly a bit nervous. "And…if you guys don't need me for anything else right now, I'm going to go get my guitar, try to find some sheet music online, and—you know—prepare."

"Of course," Rick said. Then met her eyes to say, "Thank you for doing this."

"No problem—you have to have music at your wedding, after all."

She turned to go—only to have Tanner reach out and grab her hand, giving it a squeeze. "Thank you, Jos."

She just bit her lip, sighed. "Anything for you," she whispered—then hurried away.

SHE SPENT the next hour and a half in a flurry—figuring out

what on the list she knew how to play, and what else she could fill in with. In all her years, she'd never performed at a wedding. She practiced singing "Annie's Song" and "The First Time Ever I Saw Your Face," trying to expel a little of the natural twang from her voice and hoping the whole sound wouldn't be too country for the bride's taste.

Half an hour before the wedding, as guests started to arrive at the last minute venue, the last minute musician sat down in a chair on the edge of the stage and began to play and sing. She watched Tanner and Jace serve as ushers, walking guests to the half-log seats they probably hadn't quite expected to be sitting on today. Every so often, she'd catch Tanner looking at her, too. Once he mouthed, *thank you.*

Josie couldn't have been more grateful that Elvis's "I Can't Help Falling in Love With You" had once been part of her repertoire, so she knew how to play it with ease, and as the bride began to descend the aisle, escorted by her great aunt in lieu of a deceased dad, Josie played the chords as meaning-fully and touchingly as she could, just hoping she was hitting the right note—literally—for Tanner's brother's wedding.

It was moving to watch Rick—usually gruff and intimi-dating—get a little misty as he took his vows. And the bride, Mia, was stunning and equally as emotional as she told him he was the man she wanted to spend every day of her life with, forever. Josie's chest tightened, taking it all in. And of course wishing she could have something that grand with Tanner—the way it should have been.

She'd never felt so relieved as when she'd played them back down the aisle with an acoustic version of "Happy Together" by The Turtles. Because she'd survived and not messed anything up here.

A reception was to follow at the Rose Tavern, but people lingered around the stage and benches, and some approached her to say hello and tell her they'd enjoyed her music. Hmm, she'd never seen herself as a wedding singer type, but she'd actually enjoyed it. And maybe that would be another way to turn her passion into income if needed. She was learning to be flexible about her dreams.

She was putting her guitar back in its case when she heard Tanner say, "Josie," and looked up to find him standing right in front of her. "That was amazing—you did a great job."

His smile lit up her heart—how could she not return it? "Thank you. I'm so glad I could help—and that I didn't flub it up."

"I know it must have been hard without any prep time—and Mia loved it. So thank you again."

"Well, like I said, I'm happy to help—and anything for you."

Though the words darkened his countenance a bit. She'd gotten too serious with that. Even though she meant it and it just kept coming out—the truth. And now it made her apologize. "I'm sorry—I don't mean to make you uncomfortable. You've made your boundaries clear, and I understand. I don't like it, but I understand. And I'll try to quit saying emotional things."

At this, he just nodded. And she almost saw in his eyes what he didn't say: *You don't have to quit saying emotional things—because we're not going to be around each other, so it doesn't even matter. Today is an aberration. They'll be rare—a running-into-each-other-occasionally thing. Otherwise, I'll be keeping my distance.*

But in case she had missed that in his expression, he told her, "Nothing's changed. I still can't…"

"I know," she said quietly.

Then he pointed toward the wedding party, now convening on the stage. "I gotta go—they're taking pictures."

She nodded softly, tried to smile. "Bye, Tanner."

And as she picked up her guitar case and turned her back on the happy scene, partly to escape it and partly because she wasn't a part of this joyful group, she realized that maybe he was right—about keeping some distance between them. Since every single time she saw him, it reignited the flames inside her and started the not-having-him process all over again.

And if he didn't want her enough to even try to trust her —well, then maybe the connection between them wasn't worth anything anymore anyway. She'd never stop loving him, but maybe he'd actually stopped loving her a long time ago—for driving away from him in the night.

CHAPTER ELEVEN

*S*he lowered her guitar case to the front porch and walked to the mailbox as wedding goers departed beyond the picket fence. They were all headed to a big party celebrating love—but for her it had just turned back into another Saturday, so she might as well check the mail.

She found an electric bill and...an envelope bearing the return address of the music publisher she'd signed with a few years ago in Nashville. Hmm—why was he contacting her? Their contract had been brief and led to nothing, after all.

She ripped it open and found a letter, which she skimmed. But then she stopped to read it more carefully, focusing on certain parts.

I hope this reaches you—it's been returned to me by the post office twice, but I found a new address for you, so fingers crossed.

"A Thousand Broken Hearts" and three of your other songs were used by up-and-comer Vance Mulvaney on his first album, which released in January. "A Thousand Broken Hearts" has gotten some radio play locally here in Nashville as well.

I'm happy to present your first royalty check—they'll likely get bigger as the music is distributed more widely.

Contact me if this reaches you so I'll know the address is good. And if you're interested in signing with me again for the lease of future work, let's talk.

Shell-shocked, she realized a check was indeed stapled to the back of the letter—in the amount of nine hundred and thirty-two dollars.

She couldn't believe it. Her song, her sad little song written so many years ago, had been recorded by someone! And it was being played on the radio! She kept reading the words over and over, trying to make sure she wasn't misunderstanding them. It seemed too amazing to be true.

"Pardon me, ma'am?"

She looked up to find a red-haired guy she didn't know standing a few feet away. She wondered if she was smiling dumbly and if he wondered why. "Yes?" She *was* smiling, she could feel it—she couldn't *not* smile.

"I don't know if you remember me—I was a couple years ahead of you in school—name's Rowdy Cutler."

She blinked, a little confused—and overwhelmed at the moment. "Um...maybe." Not really, but the name seemed vaguely familiar.

"I sure did enjoy your singing today."

"Oh—thank you."

"And I've been coming to your shows since you started 'em, too. They're great, exactly what this town needs—and you have a voice like an angel."

She tilted her head kindly, beginning to realize Rowdy Cutler was preparing to ask her out. And that she was probably misleading him by the fact that she couldn't wipe this stupid smile off her face—she'd barely had a chance to start absorbing this incredible news before he'd approached. She had to let him down easy, but her mind was in a whirl. *Stop smiling. Be kind, and gracious, but stop smiling.* Only she couldn't. Even if a guy she felt no attraction to was flirting with her, even if the guy she loved was doing just the opposite and had pretty much given her the heave ho. The letter in her hand was such a supreme validation that no matter how she tried, she couldn't stop beaming at poor Rowdy like a fool.

~

TANNER WAS TRYING to listen to the photographer's directions as they took group photos, first on the stage he'd built, and now out in the yard. "Groomsman two," the guy said, addressing him that way since he'd yet to pick up on his actual name, "eyes over here, toward the camera please."

Yep, fair enough thing to ask for—but damn if his attention didn't keep going up the hill to where Josie stood with… was that Rowdy Cutler, the guy who'd sold them the race car? And what the hell was happening—was he putting the moves on her? And why was she smiling at him so damn big?

"Groomsman two," the guy with the camera said again. He was really starting to get on Tanner's nerves.

"Dude," Jace admonished him under his breath, "focus or we'll never get done here. And I'm ready for a drink."

"Is that Rowdy Cutler up there talking to Josie?" he said by way of reply.

It was Rick who answered. "Think so—but look at the camera, bro."

"Is he, like, asking her out?" Tanner muttered.

"What does it matter?" Jace asked. "You're not interested in her—let her live her life, for God's sake."

"You're not interested in the girl who sang for us?" Mia piped up to say. "Why on earth not? She seems fabulous." Apparently Rick hadn't filled her in on their history while dealing with all the wedding drama.

But Tanner barely heard the people speaking to him—he

was too glued to the scene taking place by Josie's front gate. Damn, she looked so happy talking to Rowdy. To Rowdy, of all people—a decent guy but nobody's idea of a ladies' man and, in his opinion, not her type. Because her type was...him.

Her type was *him*. Only *him*. Always.

"I'm so stupid," he heard himself murmur.

"That's taking it a little far," Shelby said. "But if you can just look at the camera, we can get through this."

Because it suddenly seemed stupid to...to be so afraid of this thing with her. Because...what was that fear getting him? Just a different kind of misery.

Sure—if he took a chance with her, tried starting over with her, he might well end up miserable again. But if he *didn't* take a chance, he ensured it. Just like in her song about the thousand broken hearts.

And as much as he and the rest of the world often maligned her for throwing caution to the wind and haphazardly following her whims, there were actually ways that he admired that in her. He admired that she lived life with no regrets. That she sought joy and fulfillment. That she didn't let fear hold her back. And...hell—maybe it was time to follow her example and just do what felt right in the moment, no holds barred—right in front of everyone. For better or worse.

And just as the photographer was saying with great frustration, "Groomsman two!" Tanner left the wedding party and went charging up the hill.

"What the hell?" Rick could be heard saying behind him, as Mia asked, "Where on earth is he going? I need wedding party pictures, Tanner!"

But he couldn't stop what he'd just put into motion any more than he could have stopped Josie from going to Nashville seven years ago.

"What the hell's going on over here?" he boomed upon reaching Josie and Rowdy.

"Well, hey there, Tanner," Rowdy said. "I'm just getting to know Josie here a little better."

Rowdy was a perfectly nice guy—but that didn't stop the steam Tanner practically felt blowing out his ears. He shifted his gaze to Josie—who looked like a perfect spring day in that pretty yellow dress. "And what the hell are you smiling about?"

"Huh?"

Perhaps he should back off, make some sense, be clearer here—but he was operating on anger and instinct. "You keep smiling at him—smiling at him like he hung the damn moon or something."

"Oh," she said, finally seeming to understand the issue. Then she smiled again—at him this time, which felt much better. "I'm not smiling at *him* so much as just smiling while I talk to him because I just got some great news."

He blinked, caught off-guard by her reply. "*What* news?"

She held out a piece of paper he hadn't even noticed in her hand up to now. "Remember that music publisher I told you about? Tanner, he sold some of my songs! And they've been recorded! Not by me, but still—'A Thousand Broken Hearts' is on the radio in Nashville! How amazing is that? And he sent me a check and says there will be more!"

Tanner's eyes flew open wide. "Really?"

She nodded enthusiastically. "Really! I'm so happy!"

"That's great, Jos!" And without thinking, he picked her up and spun her around in his arms, the skirt of that yellow dress flaring in the breeze behind her. When he put her down, it occurred to him to ask, "This doesn't mean you're going back to Nashville, does it?"

"No way." She shook her head emphatically.

And then he decided to cut to the chase—before his

brother flayed him alive for messing up one more aspect of his wedding. "Then I've got some news, too."

Her eyes widened prettily. "What's that?"

"That I never stopped loving you, either, and I want to give us another chance."

At this, her breath went thready from the shock—her expression almost one of disbelief, and he guessed he could understand why. So he added, "If you can forgive me for taking this long to realize that's what I want."

She bit her lip, nodded. Looked as if she might start weeping. "You had every right."

"Don't cry," he told her. "No more tears. We've had enough to be sad about—let's be happy." And with that, he lifted both his hands to her face and kissed her.

"Bro—really?" Rick's voice sounded in his ear.

It was all he could do to stop kissing the woman he loved —but he turned, Josie still in his embrace, to see that Rick had followed him up here.

"You're kinda stealing my thunder here," his older brother said. "I don't really care, but for Mia, it's her big day, you know?"

"Fair enough," Tanner said. "Tell you what, give me two minutes, and then I'll finish the pictures."

Rick rolled his eyes. "Sure, whatever. Just trying to have a damn wedding here, that's all."

Tanner took Josie's hand, Rowdy's presence all but forgotten now, and led her up onto the porch, out of sight of the wedding party. Where he dropped to one knee, took her hand in his, and said, "Marry me, Jos?"

"Are you sure?" she asked. "This fast?"

"I've been wanting to make you my wife since we were teenagers, so it's not fast at all. And I trust in us—in you. I need you to know that. This is what I want. Will you marry me?"

He looked up to see tears rolling down her face despite his asking her not to cry, but he was pretty sure they were happy ones, so that made it okay. "For real this time," she told him.

"For real this time," he affirmed.

As he got to his feet, she threw her arms around his neck and whispered in his ear, "I'll never leave you, Tanner, ever. I promise. You're officially stuck with me forever."

EPILOGUE

TWO YEARS LATER

*O*n a steamy summer Friday night in Sassafras, South Carolina, Josie Bell Rose peeked out at the crowd from her spot behind the Rosebud Stage. Full house, as always. And a few butterflies in her stomach just before she went on—as always. Maybe more than usual tonight, though. Tonight was special. Things were changing again.

Though with so many changes in her life over the past couple of years, she should probably be used to them by now.

She and Tanner had kept their engagement secret for a while—partly so as not to further draw attention from Rick and Mia on their wedding day, and partly so no one would think they were moving too quickly after all that had happened. They began dating quietly, working through old issues, learning to trust, getting to know each other again. And at Christmastime that same year, they announced their engagement around the Rose family Christmas tree.

They'd gotten married the following April in Rosebud's backyard. Not on the stage—she didn't want to copy anyone else's wedding, wanted to make it her own. And the grounds were so beautiful, still blooming with all the colors and greenery her father had put here, that it seemed the perfect place for many reasons. Only family attended, gathered around a white arbor covered with pink rosebuds. The music at the simple but elegant ceremony had been only instrumental—she'd hired the same harpist who'd been slated to play at Rick and Mia's wedding. She made one exception, though, singing to Tanner during the ceremony a slower version of Randy Travis's classic, "Forever and Ever, Amen."

The Rosebud Stage was a bona fide success. Josie constantly auditioned acts who wanted to perform there with her. She now had a small staff to help her run the place, a website with online ticket sales, and Tanner's crew had added bathrooms and a concession stand.

Tanner had moved in to Rosebud with her when they'd married—to make it a real home again. Of course, sometimes that part went slower than she wanted—between managing and singing at the Rosebud Stage and writing new songs, many of which her music publisher had since leased to Nashville artists—she stayed busy.

And life was about to get even busier—but in a wonderful way.

"Ladies and gentlemen, please welcome to the stage our own Josie Bell."

She stepped up onto the stage Tanner had built for her with a smile as the crowd applauded her arrival. "Welcome. Welcome, everybody, to the Rosebud Stage." She looked out on the log benches, taking in some of the faces. "I see a lot of friends here tonight—and some new folks, too. Glad you came out to join us on this beautiful Sassafras evening." She spotted Jace and Shelby—and Daphne and Mitch had come up tonight, as well. The main face she sought, though, was situated in the very first row—her sweet, sexy husband.

"I want to start tonight's show with my own personal version of an old song I've always loved but never performed

107

—and I want to dedicate it to my husband who is right down in front tonight." She pointed in his general direction—then sat down on a solitary stool and strummed on her guitar the first notes of Loggins and Messina's "Danny's Song."

She looked at Tanner as she sang, the lyrics coming from her heart, and wondered how long it would take him—or anyone else—to catch on to just how special this dedication was, or that the song was about becoming a family, having a child.

Around the end of the first verse, he started looking at her a little funny, his expression full of questions. And by the time she reached the third, smiling sweetly as she sang, his eyes had turned glassy with emotion. When she finished, she leaned the guitar against her stool and walked down to him, reaching out for both his hands. He stood up, gazing into her eyes, as she said, "That's my way of telling you we're having a baby."

He blinked, one lone tear rolling down his cheek as he grinned. "Really, Jos?"

She nodded, smiled. "Really. He or she will be here by Christmas."

He let out a laugh and said, "That's amazing." Then he yelled out to the crowd at large, "We're having a baby! I'm gonna be a dad!" They all applauded, Jace and Daphne making their way down for hugs.

"You might have been the last of your brothers to marry," she told him with a wink, "but you'll be the first to have a baby Rose."

As she got back up on the stage to continue the show, she couldn't stop thinking about dreams and safety nets and how life had a way of working itself out. When she'd left for Nashville, she couldn't have imagined the life she led now. She hadn't gotten the dream she'd chased, but she'd somehow been led to an even better one—because she

couldn't imagine being happier or more fulfilled. Though…
she had a feeling a baby might change that—delivering to her
more fulfillment still.

And funny thing—if she'd never left Sassafras in the first
place, well…her life would be entirely different now in ways
she couldn't even imagine. Everything happened for a
reason, and it was easy to see in hindsight that everything
had happened in her life exactly as it was supposed to. Her
safety nets had appeared where and when she'd least
expected them, and now they held her tight.

As tight as she was going to hold Tanner and their child,
forever. Forever and ever, amen.

~

~

ABOUT THE AUTHOR

Toni Blake's love of writing began when she won an essay contest in the fifth grade. Soon after, she penned her first novel, nineteen notebook pages long. Since then, Toni has become a RITA™-nominated author of more than twenty contemporary romance novels, her books have received the National Readers Choice Award and Bookseller's Best Award, and her work has been excerpted in *Cosmo*. Toni lives in the Midwest and enjoys traveling, crafts, and spending time outdoors.

Learn more about Toni and her books at:
www.toniblake.com

facebook.com/AuthorToniBlake

twitter.com/AuthorToniBlake

instagram.com/AuthorToniBlake

Made in the USA
Middletown, DE
02 November 2020